SEBERIAN™

THE HIDDEN BATTLE REVEALED

J. R. DAHL

ISBN: 0996459901
ISBN 13: 9780996459907
Library of Congress Control Number: 2015909355
Published by 2617 Publishing LLC

DEDICATION

This book is dedicated to my girls.

Glossary

Lonan

- Mechanical Engineer of the planet Helion (specializing in Aerospace & Aircraft design)
- Husband of Averine
- Brother of Sevran
- Childhood friend of Telgrin

Averine

- High-ranking Medial Officer in the Helion army (Field medic)
- Daughter of Kilgron
- Wife of Lonan

Kilgron

- Supreme Commander of the planet Helion
- Long-time warrior in the Helion Army (severely wounded in battle)
- Father of Averine

Sevran

- Commanding officer of Helion Army Field Medical Units.
- Brother of Lonan
- Childhood friend of Telgrin
- Single and very popular with the ladies of Helion

Telgrin

- Mechanical Engineer of the planet Helion (specializing in weapon and transportation systems)
- Socially awkward but brilliant engineer
- Classmate of Lonan at Helion Military Academy

Maginon

- CEO of Nemaron Corp.

Devakin

- Ruthless Commander of Leviathan Army
- Powerful and experienced warrior

Armon

- Commander of Seberian Forces
- Long-time warrior
- Father of Ahren and Cloin

Ahren

- Young leader of Seberian Forces
- Powerful, disciplined warrior, especially gifted at covert operations
- Son of Armon
- Brother of Cloin

Cloin

- Young leader of Seberian Forces
- Incredibly focused and intelligent warrior, especially gifted in hand-to-hand combat
- Daughter of Armon
- Sister of Ahren

Nemaron

- Intergalactic Corporation that sells rare minerals and essential commodities

Leviathan

- Mysterious supernatural Army

Seberians

- Small elite supernatural force of humans

Heliender s

- Soldiers of the planet Helion

Satan

- Demon, former Angel (Angelic name = Lucifer)
- Chief of all Demons
- As an Angel one of the nine chief (or Arch) angels

Mammon

- Demon, former Angel (Angelic name = Mammelel)
- Direct subordinate to Satan while they were Angels

Abaddon

- Demon, former Angel (Angelic name = Abadol)
- As an angel one of the nine chief (or Arch) angels

Abadile

- Demon, former Angel (Angelic name = Abafrile)
- As an Angel one of the nine chief (or Arch) angels

Tekel

- Chief (or Arch) angel, one of the original nine
- Strongest and wisest of the Angels
- Commander over all of God's faithful Angels

Balim

- Chief (or Arch) angel, one of the original nine
- Guardian over galaxies 55x5 through 78x35

Genon

- Subordinate Angel
- Had been a direct subordinate to Satan before his fall
- The only Angel under Satan's command to not succumb to temptation
- Was direct witness to the beginning of war in Heaven

Chapter 1

The planet Tarnus orbited a small star in the outer ridges of galaxy 55X9. It was densely populated, and its cities were so well lit that their outlines could be seen from a long distance out into space.

One night, six massive carrier ships and hundreds of well-armed fighter shuttles entered its atmosphere. As they closed in on the planet, they triggered an alarm system within the Tarnus planetary-defense center.

"Commander, we have activity in sector fifteen," reported a soldier as he monitored the outer defense system from deep in the heart of the command center. The room was filled with thirty other soldiers, but none seemed to take much notice of what he had said.

"Show me," the commander replied as he sipped from his mug of Crulian coffee and walked toward the center of the room.

The soldier punched some keys, and an image appeared on the main screen on the wall of the command center. The image showed the six carriers and hundreds of fighter shuttles, which quickly drew everyone's attention.

A table in the center of the room projected holographic images of the ships. The computer system immediately began to analyze them and their weapons' capabilities. As it continued to find and outline more and more weapons, the look on the commander's face became noticeably uneasy. He was a seasoned veteran, and not many things scared him, but this fleet sent a chill down his spine.

"Begin transmission!" barked the commander. "Vessels, be aware you are entering Tarnus's atmosphere. Identify yourselves immediately!"

They waited in silence, with no response.

"This doesn't look good. Sound the alarm. Get our fighters in the air, and prepare surface-to-air missiles."

Outside of the command center, a full moon lit up the runways as the alarm sounded and pilots scrambled to their waiting fighters. Ground troops jumped into armored transports and tanks and took off in the direction of the invaders approaching from the far side of the capital city that lay between them. In the clear night sky, they could see the enormous carriers hovering out in space and the swarm of fighters that looked like a storm cloud descending on the city.

Hundreds of fighter jets were launched from electromagnetic rails that ran along the ground and then tapered up into the air. After they left the rails, they fired their main engines and took off into the outer atmosphere. Around the perimeter of the base, enormous surface-to-air cannons turned and took aim.

Inside the control room, the computer locked onto incoming fighters. "Cannons locked and ready to fire, sir," reported one of the soldiers.

"On my mark."

Outside of the base, many more fighters took off from the rails and from bunkers buried underground. Thousands of them now filled the night sky. One of the pilots reported in: "Unit one ready to engage. We're waiting on your orders, sir."

Back in the control room, everyone anxiously watched the main screen as the intruders continued to draw near. "Identify yourself immediately, or we will open fire," ordered the commander.

They sat in silence with no reply.

Aboard the command ship of the intruding army, a group of soldiers piloted the carrier as others called in orders to their fighters. The captain sat in the middle of the command bridge. He smiled as the transmission from the planet ended and he watched their fighters fly out to meet him. He was dressed in a nonmilitary black suit, and his soldiers were dressed in dark-gray flight uniforms. Like his soldiers, his skin was pale and his eyes dark and sunken.

"Launch the catalyst," he ordered.

Missile tubes opened on the front of each carrier, from which two enormous missiles were launched.

Back at the Tarnus base, another alarm sounded. "Sir, they've launched missiles," reported a nervous soldier.

"All units open fire! Launch countermeasures!"

The cannons shook the ground as their barrels retracted and fired multiple missiles. "All fighter units engage! Fire at will!" shouted the commander.

The Tarnus fighters released a wall of rounds at the intruder missiles. They were surprised to see that their rounds had no effect. Some of the fighters circled around to take another shot at the missiles while the rest headed toward the intruders.

"Leave the missiles for our countermeasures. All units engage their fighters!" shouted the commander as he anxiously paced back and forth through the command center. The fighters pulled away as the catalyst missiles headed for a collision with the Tarnus countermeasures. The missiles impacted with a tremendous explosion that lit up the night sky. Everyone in the control room cheered.

Then the commander's mug hit the floor, spilling his drink, as he stood and stared at the screen. The entire room went silent in amazement. The intruder missiles flew out of the cloud of the explosion, still on course to hit the planet. The Tarnus missiles had done nothing. A nearly palpable fear seemed to pass its way across the room.

The captain of the invading army smiled as he watched hundreds of missiles and fighters coming toward his ships. "Activate the catalysts."

One of his soldiers punched some keys, and moments later, the intruder missiles exploded simultaneously, emitting shock waves that covered the entire planet and extended out into space.

The Tarnus fighters and missiles lost power as the shock waves reached them. All their electrical and propulsion systems shut down. The fighters floated in space, and the missiles began to fall back to the planet.

Inside the cockpits of their fighters, the Tarnus pilots scrambled as they tried to restart their ships. They began to suffocate as their oxygen-supply systems shut down and they quickly used up what little air they had left.

Back on the planet, the shock waves wiped out all power to whatever they came in contact with. The military command center went completely black, as was the nearby capital city. Their own missiles became a threat as they plummeted back to the planet and exploded on impact, taking out buildings and military vehicles in the process.

"Launch first-wave ground assault," ordered the intruder's captain as he settled back into his command chair.

The sides of the command ship opened, and hundreds of attack fighters and bulky cargo ships poured out. As they flew toward the planet, they shot down and destroyed the helpless Tarnus fighters floating in space. From their position, they could see the shock waves passing across the surface of the planet, leaving complete darkness in their paths.

In the Tarnus command center, all the lights were out except for dim emergency lighting. The soldiers scrambled around the room, trying to regain power.

"Sir, all communications are out."

"Send two units to the power plant to help get us back online," ordered the commander.

Outside of the command center, the only light that could be seen was the pale moonlight and explosions from Tarnus's own missiles hitting the ground. Thirty armed soldiers ran out of the command center as hundreds more emerged from their barracks. They looked up into the night sky to see the intruder fighters destroying their pilots and descending on the planet like a swarm of locusts. The soldiers ran to the nearest armored transports and climbed in, only to find that the shock waves had knocked out their power as well.

"Sir, all transports are dead," reported one of the drivers.

"We'll go on foot. Move out to the power station!" barked an infantry commander.

The soldiers ran toward a large building two kilometers off in the distance. When they arrived, they found men scrambling around the outside the building, which appeared to be in perfect condition. The infantry commander grabbed one of the plant workers and asked, "What's going on?"

"We don't know. All the reactors shut down at the same time. We've never seen anything like this."

Off in the distance, the intruder's fighters and cargo ships continued their decent into the capital city. Several of their fighters flew down in advance of the main squadron. They flew very low and began to fire down probes that they strategically spaced two to three kilometers apart. These probes were long shafts with sharp, pointed ends that penetrated deep into the ground. They stood nearly six meters tall. Mounted on their tops were massive globes that were filled with a deep-red mist that pulsated with an intense light. The globes were encased in ancient-looking black metal scrollwork. They pulsed in unison as they lined the streets.

At the far end of the city, the Tarnus commander was assembling thousands of his soldiers. They barricaded themselves behind vehicles in the streets as they took aim at the invader ships. As those dropping the probes came near, someone yelled, "INCOMING!"

"Bring them down!" shouted the commander.

The soldiers with shoulder-mounted rocket launchers took aim and pulled the triggers, only nothing happened. They examined their weapons to try to figure out what was wrong. Again they tried, but still, the weapons were useless. The rest of the soldiers lifted their rifles and tried to fire, but nothing. Dread overtook them as, one by one, they realized that the invader's missiles had negated all their defenses.

"Prepare for hand-to-hand combat!" shouted the commander as he tried to rally his courage. They all pulled half-meter-long blades from the sides of their rifles and attached them to the ends of the barrels.

The intruder cargo ships fired landing engines as they slowly touched down throughout the city. Ramps extended down from the bottom of their hulls while the Tarnus soldiers tried to prepare themselves. The largest cargo ship landed nearest to the Tarnus line of defense. Down the ramp walked a huge soldier dressed in black body armor. This was the commander of the intruder army, and they called him Devakin.

He was followed by hundreds of soldiers armed with rifles. They all wore heavy black body armor and helmets with complete face masks. Their armor was so formidable that it looked as though it could withstand a direct missile impact. Stretched across their chest plates were boomerang-shaped red lights that pulsated in unison with the red probes that now covered the city.

Devakin stood out due to gray metal strips down the shoulders of his battle armor, which indicated his high rank. He was the only one in his army not wearing a face mask. He stood well over two meters tall, and his face was a sickly pale gray. His eyes appeared sunken as the skin around them was filled with deep-blue veins that seemed to crawl underneath his skin. The whites of his eyes were also filled with thin blue veins. His soldiers continued to pour out of the cargo ships and were followed by massive armored transports.

From behind the barricade, the Tarnus soldiers were overcome with doubt as they watched these massive soldiers preparing for battle. The once powerful and experienced warriors were now trembling with intense fear. They had fought countless enemies, but there was something different about this army—something that seemed to grip them deep inside their chests.

The Tarnus commander pulled them abruptly back to reality as he yelled, "Attack!" They jumped out from behind the vehicles where they had been hiding and charged the intruder army. The wave of soldiers broke against the intruders like ocean waves crashing against rocky shores. They swung in desperation, as they knew their blades were the last defense between this army and their people.

The intruders set aside their rifles and met them in hand-to-hand combat. They seemed eager for the chance to engage in a close-quarters fight. Every thrust of the Tarnus soldiers' blades was dodged with ease. The speed of the intruders was incredible. They moved four times faster than a normal man. The Tarnus soldiers tried desperately to land a strike with their blades, only to hit nothing but air.

The intruders toyed with them like this awhile until it became obvious they were growing tired. Once the Tarnus soldiers were weary, the intruders quickly and easily disarmed the desperate soldiers. In a whirlwind of broken arms, legs, and necks, the intruders drove through their lines. The intruder army moved with tremendous speed and power while the Tarnus soldiers were absolutely powerless against them.

The Tarnus commander faced off against Devakin. Every strike of his blade was dodged until he finally landed a blow that cut the massive warrior across the right bicep. The blade laid open his flesh. Devakin didn't flinch. He laughed as the wound bled profusely for a few seconds and then mysteriously healed itself.

The Tarnus commander was amazed and paused for a second as he stood confused. Devakin grabbed him by the throat and lifted him in the air as if he weighed nothing. The commander kicked and gasped for air as he tried to free himself. One of his kicks landed in his attacker's face.

That seemed to trigger the end of what had looked like playtime. With just one hand, Devakin snapped the commander's neck and threw his body thirty meters back behind the Tarnus lines. His twisted body landed beside five soldiers still hiding behind the cover of the vehicles. As they looked down at the lifeless body, they realized that they had absolutely no hope to defeat this army.

High atop the tallest building in the city, the Tarnus president stood with his wife and daughter as they looked down from the balcony of their home and watched the attack on their people. The daughter and wife were visibly shaken as they held each other. The president turned to them and said, "Don't worry. I've made a deal that assures that we'll be well taken care of."

As he said this, a shadow moved behind him while the veins in the whites of his eyes turned a blackish blue and then back to white.

"What have you done?" asked his wife as realization and horror passed over her face.

On top of the building, an intruder fighter slowed as it came in for a landing. Four armed Tarnus soldiers and the president's assistant walked out onto the landing pad. The loading ramp of the shuttle opened, and five men walked out. The captain of the intruder army had gotten off his command ship and was now being escorted by four of his soldiers. The president's assistant nervously approached and, with a tremble in his voice, said, "We've been waiting for you Maginon, sir."

Maginon continued on without turning to look at him. He walked through the doors on the edge of the landing pad and into the hallway that led to the president's home.

"No one else knows of our arrangement; is that correct?" Maginon asked as he continued down the hall, still not bothering to turn his attention to the assistant.

"Yes, sir, that's right," he replied as he trailed behind like a dog begging for approval. The men entered the president's main living chamber to find him and his family waiting.

"It looks like all is going as planned," said the president of Tarnus as he tried not to choke on his words.

"Yes, it is. Thank you again for your help. Now for your reimbursement."

Maginon pulled a handgun from inside his jacket and shot the president through the heart. The girls screamed as they huddled together. The president's assistant jumped in fear but took no action. The Tarnus soldiers with him also made no move to defend their leader but stood at attention. Maginon then turned to his soldiers and said, "Finish this for me," as he walked back around the corner and down the hall.

The women cried and huddled around the president as he lay dying on the floor. His assistant stood for a moment, staring at the family with a look of grief. He then turned and ran out of the room and followed Maginon.

At that moment, the intruder soldiers turned and opened fire on the president's guards. As they hit the floor, the president's assistant turned back in disbelief. He then ran and caught up with the captain as he stepped out onto the landing pad.

"But sir, my guards?"

Back in the room, he could hear the women's screams grow louder. There were two more shots and then silence. The assistant stopped and looked back in horror while Maginon's soldiers made their way back down the hall.

"You've done me a great favor. Your people will serve me well. But I don't think that I'll need anymore of your help," said Maginon as he walked up the ramp into his waiting shuttle.

Still stunned by the execution of the women, the assistant nearly whispered, "But, sir?"

"Thank you, that will be all. Fire." Seconds later a blast came from the hull of the ship that ripped through the assistant's chest and killed him instantly. Maginon didn't flinch as he walked up the ramp. His soldiers followed behind him. Moments later the ramp closed, and the ship took off into the night sky.

Meanwhile, back in the center of the city, all the citizens of Tarnus were being dragged down to the streets. Hundreds of thousands of people had their hands bound and were being loaded into various transports. Devakin stood on the wing of his shuttle as he supervised the progress. In the background, women and children could be heard crying and screaming for help. Wives screamed for their husbands and children as they were separated and loaded into different vehicles. Some of the families wouldn't separate, so soldiers forced them apart.

"Continue scanning the buildings. We wouldn't want to leave anyone behind. Especially her," said Devakin as he pointed down to a beautiful young woman in line. "You know where she goes."

A solider pulled the woman out of line and away from her husband. "No! Let her stay with me!" yelled the man as he tried to wrestle her from the soldier's grip. But he was no match for the intruder's abnormal strength. Another soldier punched him in the face and knocked him unconscious. The woman screamed for her husband as they picked her up and carried her to a shuttle that they were loading exclusively with young women.

Just then a very muscular man tried to defend his family against a particularly aggressive soldier. He was easily thrown aside by a soldier who then pulled his weapon and shot him. His wife screamed as she ran over and hugged his dying body.

Devakin jumped down from the wing of the shuttle and landed beside the soldier. He punched him in the side of the face and said, "No killing. You don't get paid anything for dead bodies."

"Yes, sir."

Suddenly the planet quaked from an impact. Several kilometers outside the city, a shuttle landed. It had a massive drill bit in the center of its hull. It anchored itself with legs that impaled spikes into the ground while three more identical shuttles neared the planet.

Immediately after the first shuttle anchored itself, the drill bit started to rotate and, within seconds, was several meters below the surface. On the top of the shuttle sat the control room, which was a heavily armored cockpit with small porthole-shaped windows. Inside this control room sat five soldiers. The officer of the shuttle radioed to Devakin: "I'll need five thousand volunteers for drill duty."

Back in the center of the city, Devakin replied, "They're on their way." He pointed to soldiers loading one of the ground transports and yelled, "Five thousand to the mines as soon as they're loaded."

Moments later, the intruders closed the loading ramp of the transport before it rolled out in the direction of the drill shuttles.

Chapter 2

On the opposite side of galaxy 55X9, the planet Helion orbited within a small binary-star system. The planet was covered in steep, snow-covered mountain ranges and beautiful green valleys. The inhabitants called themselves Helienders. Their home in a neighboring galaxy had been taken captive. People from many nations fled as refugees and came together to settle the planet they came to call Helion. When they arrived, they found it completely uninhabited, yet what they did find were ancient ruins in the form of great caverns and tunnels built underneath one of the low-lying mountain ranges.

They thoroughly searched the entire system of caves, looking for any signs of the inhabitants. They found nothing; there were no skeletal remains or dead bodies. In fact, they found no signs of war or death at all. It looked as though they had simply decided to take everything and move. What they did find, however, was a combination of natural caves and caverns that had been masterfully connected to create a vast underground dwelling. These enormous caverns were reinforced with beautiful handcrafted stone columns. Tunnels led deep under the mountain to large underground rivers and waterfalls. They tested the water and found it to be extremely clean and well suited for drinking. The caverns were so large that their entire new civilization was able to live in this underground sanctuary, with plenty of room to grow.

With no one else to lay claim on the underground home, the Helienders made it their own. They were very resourceful and gifted with abilities to create and engineer in ways that allowed them to work with their environment. They blended their advanced technologies into their new home. They reinforced the ancient stone columns of the caverns with specially formulated steel alloy framing and turned the great halls into hangars for their spacecraft.

This allowed the Helienders to hide themselves and all their people from the possibility of being found by the evil force that had driven them from their original homes. Their entire civilization was able to hide from any possible probes or satellites passing by the planet. They didn't build any homes in the green valleys but instead confined their habitation entirely to the mountain. Some of their living quarters lined the outer parts of the mountain, which had small porthole windows that allowed sunlight to enter.

In the deeper caverns, they built light-transfer systems that absorbed sunlight high on top of the mountain and then piped it in. This ensured that all living areas had natural light. It also allowed them to conserve energy for lighting. They used their sun's energy to power most of their needs. They also pulled heat from deep within the core of the planet.

The Helienders found this particularly important due to the position of their planet, as it orbited the primary star in their binary-star system. The two stars were very similar in mass and, therefore, traveled in long elliptical orbits that focused on one common center of mass. Helion orbited what they calculated to be the primary star, as its mass and gravitational pull was slightly greater. Helion was located in a very suitable position to sustain life. However, based on the combination of the star's orbit and the planet's orbit around the primary star, they experienced very extreme weather patterns every ten years. It was at these times that there were long periods of heavy snowfall followed by an extended time of heavy rain and cloud cover. Pulling heat from the planet's core became particularly important during this time. The planet then emerged from this cold season with tremendous plant growth.

At the midway point of the ten-year orbit, the Helienders' star brought them very close to the secondary star in their system, which created more extreme heat. The melting snow from the long winter years created large lakes in the valleys below the Helienders' mountain home. Immense green forests that crept right up to the edge of the lakes covered the valleys.

Not long after the attack on planet Tarnus, two men riding armored military motorcycles emerged from the Helion forest trails. They raced along the path with tremendous speed and nimbleness as they glided across the rough terrain. They quickly glanced over their shoulders as they approached a small ravine. They were being followed. The ravine was thirty meters wide and had a mound of dirt that stood another two meters tall along the left side of the trail. Without hesitation, they accelerated up the mound and jumped the ravine. As they flew thirty meters through the air, they again looked back over their shoulders, trying to catch a glimpse of their pursuer, before turning forward just seconds before landing on the far side. Moments later a four-wheeled off-road attack vehicle appeared on the far side of the ravine. It was heavily armored with a dual gun turret mounted on the top and missile-launching cannons on the sides. It had open wheel wells and very large tires. Its suspension had a great deal of travel, which allowed it absorb the rough trail. It also didn't slow down as it approached the edge of the ravine and hit the mound of dirt, launching into the air.

The second motorcycle soldier looked down at the computer console mounted just behind the base of his handlebars. The console projected a holographic image of the attack vehicle following them as it touched down on their side of the ravine. Just then they turned a corner in the trail and found themselves out of the woods and riding across a beach clearing beside an enormous lake. There was no other trail out of the clearing, so they raced down to the edge of the water and turned the motorcycles to face their pursuer.

Seconds later the attack vehicle emerged from the trail and rocketed its way across the sandy beach, heading directly toward them. It came to an abrupt stop in a cloud of dust just two meters from them. The men sat on their motorcycles and watched as the left door of the vehicle popped open and lifted vertically into the air.

"How was that?" called Averine from inside the vehicle as the engine stopped.

"I'm impressed," came Lonan's muffled voice from under his helmet.

The two soldiers dismounted their motorcycles and took off their helmets.

"Who taught you to drive like that?" asked Lonan as he walked toward the open door of the attack vehicle.

"My brother-in-law," she answered with a grin.

The second man, Sevran, laughed as he crouched down and examined his motorcycle.

Lonan reached down into the vehicle and kissed his beautiful young wife.

"Is that right? Fine. Get out of my way, I need to examine the control panel."

Lonan playfully pulled her from the driver's seat and climbed into the vehicle.

"If you want driving lessons, just let me know," said Sevran as he pulled water bottles from his backpack.

Averine smiled as he threw her a bottle.

"Driving lessons from you? No thanks," answered Lonan as he tried to examine the vehicle's onboard computer system.

"Averine, how did it handle?"

"It was great."

"You hit some of those mounds pretty hard."

"You said you wanted me to test it out."

"Yeah, but I don't want you to get hurt," said Lonan as he stepped out and walked toward her.

"You're so protective."

She reached over and kissed him on the cheek while he continued to examine data on the removable portion of the onboard control module.

"Yes, I am." He looked up from the screen for a second and gave her a very serious but loving look.

Sevran splashed water from his bottle onto the side of the engine of his motorcycle.

"Oh no! I've got a major leak on my bike."

Lonan nearly threw Averine aside as he ran over to see the problem. "What? Where? Where's it coming from?" he asked as he franticly examined the engine.

"Oh, maybe from my water bottle," said Sevran as he began to laugh.

"Idiot! Go get the refueling equipment," ordered Lonan as he cleaned the water off the engine of the motorcycle.

Sevran smiled as he walked around the back side of Averine's attack vehicle, which they called the Stinger. He opened the back compartment and took out a large case that he delivered to his brother. Lonan opened the case and set up his equipment. He took one hose from the side of the case and threw it out into the lake. He then took two other hoses from the other side and plugged them into his bike.

"This should only take a couple minutes. The vapor re-collection system is working fine; I just want to top off the tanks and test the system," said Lonan.

"How long for the Stinger?" asked Averine.

"Five minutes, tops."

"It's so good to get out of the med bay," said Sevran as he looked around and enjoyed the beautiful sun-drenched scenery.

"Yeah," agreed Averine. "Thanks for making us come with you. I needed this."

"Yeah, I don't understand how you two can stay cooped up in those labs and exam rooms with all those sickos."

"So compassionate, as usual," replied Averine.

"We call them patients," added Sevran.

"You know what I mean—all those germs and blood."

"It's OK, big bro. Not everyone is cut out to do what we do."

"Why don't you get to work on the sensors?" asked Lonan.

"You got it, boss."

Sevran flung the last of his water at Lonan as he walked again to the back of the Stinger.

"I'll help you," said Averine as she followed behind Sevran.

While Lonan continued to refuel the vehicles, Averine and Sevran carried toolboxes to a small tower just into the forest beside the shore. There they went to work on one of the many security sensors that had been strategically placed across the planet.

The lake was a beautiful deep blue, and the sun shimmered off small waves created by a calm breeze. It was a peaceful setting. The far side of the lake jumped directly up into the side of a tree-covered mountain. As the three completed their work, they were completely unaware of the fact that they were being watched from deep within the tree cover on the far side of the lake.

Back at the base, Lonan's dog, Max, walked through the door of the main hangar and looked out over the sun-covered valley below. As he looked out, his ears went up, and he gave off a half bark.

"What's going on, Max? Do you miss our friends?" asked Telgrin, Lonan's fellow engineer, as he stood at a mobile computer station punching some keys. He took a pen from behind his ear and wrote something on an electronic pad beside him. He was working in one of the labs that they referred to as "the Shop," which was located on the side of the main hangar. This is where they implemented many of their inventions and did a lot of their testing. At times it became a dangerous place.

Telgrin was a faithful friend to Lonan, Sevran, and Averine. They had all grown up together and shared a lot of history. Telgrin and Lonan had studied engineering together at the academy. They each had their strengths. Telgrin was more technical and precise, while Lonan was more creative. Everyone loved Telgrin even though he was a little socially awkward. The fact that he hid himself in the lab didn't seem to help that awkwardness.

Just then the computer nearby sounded a quiet signal: "Incoming friendly transport in sector nine."

Telgrin turned and looked at Max inquisitively. "Max, you're quicker than our sensors. I need to do something about that."

The computer projected a holographic image of the three vehicles as they traveled up the side of the mountain.

Moments later an older, distinguished-looking man hovered into the shop on a small transportation device. His name was Kilgron. He was the supreme commander of the Helion people and had once been a great warrior. One could see that time and service to his people had not been kind to his body. When he came to a stop, he stepped off the machine and limped toward Telgrin. Kilgron used a cane because his left leg was missing but had been replaced with a mechanical one. His entire left arm had also been replaced with an artificial limb, which seemed to make using the cane all that much more difficult. His body had been severely beaten, but his mind was all that much stronger.

"Shouldn't they be back by now?" he asked as he crossed the shop.

"That's them now, sir. They should be here in the next ten minutes," replied Telgrin.

"Could you please remind my daughter to meet me in the main council chamber as soon as she arrives?"

"Yes, sir. What about your son-in-law?"

Kilgron's face turned even more serious as he answered, "Keep him here. He would have no interest in this meeting."

Moments after Kilgron left, the three vehicles rolled into the hangar and parked in front of the shop. Max greeted them with his typical jumping and licking.

"Hey Max. Did you miss me?" asked Lonan as he dismounted his bike and took off his helmet.

Lonan and Sevran rolled the motorcycles to their stands. As they put the bikes in position, they stepped on switches that caused platforms to come up from the floor with stabilizing arms. These platforms lifted the bikes and made them stand upright so that they could be worked on.

As Averine stepped out of the Stinger, Telgrin yelled over to her: "My lady, your presence was requested by our noble commander of military affairs."

"What?" she yelled as she struggled to hear over the noise.

"Your dad was here. He wants you to meet him in the council chambers," yelled Telgrin.

"Really? What about me?" asked Lonan as he shut off his motorcycle, ending the noise.

Telgrin hesitated as he said, "He thought that you would probably prefer to stay here and analyze our data." Telgrin nervously grinned at Lonan.

Lonan ignored him as he walked over to speak more privately with his wife.

"Your father is calling you into a special meeting again? I bet I know what this is about."

"Maybe. Maybe not. I'll find out," she said with a mischievous look in her eye.

"You know how I feel about these missions," he snapped back with a deadly serious tone.

"I have to go. I'll meet you here afterward," she said as she walked toward the door.

Lonan lowered his head in frustration as she walked away. Out of the corner of his eye, he saw Sevran walking toward the door. "You're going too?" asked Lonan.

"Yeah, sorry, bro. I'll fill you in later," answered Sevran as he followed Averine through the door.

Lonan turned to Telgrin. "Well, I guess it's just the two of us."

"Great," answered Telgrin as he turned his head and rolled his eyes.

"Why don't you order food and have it delivered? We have a lot of data to upload," said Lonan as he jumped into the driver's seat of the Stinger.

"You got it," answered Telgrin, who actually did enjoy shop time with his childhood friend but tried to act like he had better things to do—even though everyone knew that he didn't.

Outside, the sky turned red and orange as their two suns set in the valley below. Max walked back over to the door and peered out. He looked off into the distance and let out a half bark. Something was wrong. The fur on his back stood up as he gave a low growl.

Chapter 3

Averine and Sevran entered a large dome-shaped room with a window at the very peak, which flooded the room with natural light. As they entered, they were greeted by seven men and seven women seated at a round table in the center of the room. One of the seven men was Kilgron, Averine's father. The rest were talking quietly among themselves and nodded in their direction as they entered.

The outer wall of the room was lined with tiered seating. Most of the seats were filled with military and medical officers, as well as scientists and professors from the academy. Sevran and Averine quietly slipped into seats near the front.

"Wow. The entire counsel is here. What did we do this time?" whispered Sevran.

"Relax, it's not that. If we were in trouble, my father would've scolded me himself beforehand," she whispered back.

"You don't know what this is about?"

"Not entirely. All I know is that it has to do with a planetary security risk," answered Averine.

"Well, I hope it doesn't take too long. I have two dates tonight."

"Two?"

"Yeah, two."

Averine rolled her eyes, shook her head, and said, "Your brother's right; you are an idiot."

"What?" Sevran asked with a grin.

Kilgron gave them an inquisitive look from the far side of

the table as they whispered back and forth. Another door on the opposite side of the room opened, and four soldiers entered and sat down.

"Now that everyone is here, let's begin," said Kilgron as he called everyone's attention. "The purpose of this meeting is to discuss a very dangerous situation. I'm afraid that we have a confirmed attack and takeover of yet another peaceful planet. However," he paused and looked around the room, "this one was within our own star system."

There was a collective gasp in the room as everyone turned and whispered to his or her neighbor.

"General," said Kilgron, nodding at a uniformed solider.

One of the four soldiers that had entered was General Crine. He was second in command, after Kilgron, over all military activities. He stepped up to a small podium and punched some keys in the console. A hologram appeared in the center of the round table. The first image was of the Helienders' binary-star system. It showed their two stars in orbit and highlighted the planet Helion as it traveled in its elliptical orbit around the primary star. The image then zoomed out to reveal their neighboring star systems and continued until it showed all of galaxy 55X9, which was shaped like a spiral with four very distinct arms. The computer then zoomed back into an area that was within the same arm as Helion. It highlighted a large planet and continued to zoom in until it reached Tarnus.

"Our scouts have reported that the planet Tarnus has been completely overtaken. They've found several hundred dead and thousands of captives working newly drilled mines. The invaders have already begun to strip the planet's core, and more drill shuttles continue to arrive. The rest of the population has been taken captive, but we do not know where."

As General Crine spoke, the computer scanned around the surface of the planet and showed, in outline form, what he was describing.

With this report, everyone in the room shifted uneasily in his or her chair.

"Needless to say, we're very concerned about the close proximity of this attack," added Kilgron.

Sevran leaned forward and put his head in his hands and quietly said, "You can say that again."

"The force that's operating the mines is a Nemaron detail."

Sevran asked, "What would a raw-materials company like Nemaron be doing taking over a planet?"

"The other question is, how would they have the man power to do so? Tarnus was a large and well-defended planet," added General Cline. "The answer is that they had help. Many of the smaller mercenary armies that we normally rescue captives from are now on the Nemaron payroll."

"It still doesn't seem like that would be enough soldiers to take over Tarnus," said Sevran.

Kilgron spoke up: "Nemaron has grown tremendously as of late. They not only sell raw materials and minerals, they also have begun energy sourcing and selling integrated weapons systems."

"Some of the most disturbing news is still to come," added General Cline "I'm sure that this will be a source of much discussion—it always seems to be—but it appears that one of our greatest fears has been realized. The Nemaron Corporation has apparently joined forces with a mysterious Leviathan army."

One of the young science officers interrupted: "You can't take those accounts seriously. An army of superpowered, unstoppable soldiers? I find it to be nothing more than delusions from badly wounded survivors and ancient fables."

This prompted Averine to interrupt: "Sir, with all due respect, the survivors' accounts that you are referring to can be taken seriously. The patients have not shown any indications of posttraumatic delusions. All our instruments indicate that they're telling the truth."

As a high-ranking medical officer, Averine's opinion was held in very high regard throughout Helion.

Just then, a very old professor from the academy spoke up from the back. His voice was weak and frail, but the intensity of his words pierced everyone's ears.

"Any possible accounts of Leviathan being near must not be taken lightly."

Everyone turned and looked at the man has he slowly rose from his seat.

"None of you have enough years to have spoken with those who saw the Leviathan as they drove us from our homeland. If the Leviathan have reemerged, we must take great caution."

"The fact is," interrupted General Crine, "our scouts brought back reports of a small unit of soldiers that fit the description: massive, heavily armored men who have tremendous strength and speed."

The young science officer interrupted: "How do we know that they're human? Maybe they're an alien race that we haven't yet encountered."

"What difference does that make? They're still extremely dangerous," added Sevran, who had a hard time hiding his frustration.

"We were able to trace their path out of our star system," interjected Kilgron. "For that, we should all be very thankful. However, we're particularly disturbed by what we've found. Normally the mercenary armies relocate captives to other planets with mines and work them until they're dead. But now that they are joined with Nemaron, the captives have been relocated to a facility that we have never seen before."

"Our scouts weren't able to get close enough to give full reconnaissance. But they could see that it was not a mine. They are doing something else with these people," added General Crine. He then turned to Sevran and Averine and asked, "You and Lonan were successful in upgrading all of the sensors on the western mountains, I trust."

"Yes, sir. Everything is in place and working perfectly," answered Sevran.

"Good, because we've retracted all our satellites. We don't want to call attention to ourselves. All security will be doubled from this point forward."

"Now the question that we must discuss is, what are we going to do about this?" asked Kilgron.

General Crine said, "It's my opinion that we need to complete another rescue mission. That would allow us to save many of those taken captive and get a closer look at this new threat. I would like to send my best soldiers as a security detail."

Kilgron responded, "This is a decision for the counsel, but we want the input of our chief military, medical, and scientific leaders. If any of you think that we should not move forward with a rescue mission, please speak up now."

There was a long silence until the young science officer spoke up: "I highly doubt the existence of these fabled Leviathan, but I would be eager to examine any samples of specimens that the team brought back to me."

Kilgron said, "This would, of course, be a voluntary mission. How many of you would be willing to take part?"

Averine and Sevran quickly raised their hands, as did all of the military officers. Kilgron looked at his daughter with love and pride mixed with concern as he said, "The council will now discuss the issue and vote. We will tell you of our decision at a military briefing at 0500 hours tomorrow morning. Until then we want this to be off-limits to nonmilitary personnel. Is that understood?"

Everyone responded, "Yes, sir," and then filed out of the room as the council members continued to discuss.

Back in the shop, Lonan and Telgrin continued to work on vehicles. The last bit of orange sunlight was disappearing as night took over. Lonan was working on the two motorcycles as Telgrin lay on the floor under the Stinger when Averine walked in.

"It's about time. That was a long meeting. What's going on? I've seen more patrols outside," said Lonan with an agitated tone.

"Sorry. Your brother and I stayed back to talk to General Crine after the meeting. Let's go home and talk about it. You can hit the bag and work out while I fill you in. You know how I love to watch you work out," she said as she pulled him to the door and manipulatively grinned.

"Great. This doesn't sound good. Telgrin, can you clean up for me?" asked Lonan.

"But I have plans with Sarah," Telgrin answered as he scrambled out from underneath the Stinger.

Lonan and Averine both stopped and looked at him in surprise.

"Really?" they asked in unison.

"Well, not yet. I was going to call her—never mind. I'll clean up. I have nothing else to do," whined Telgrin as he crawled back underneath the Stinger.

"No, wait. If you have plans, I'll stay and clean up."

"No, I—I'm sure she's busy."

"Are you sure?" asked Averine. "I'm sure that, if you call her, she'll say yes."

"No. I changed my mind."

"OK, let's leave him alone," said Lonan as he pulled Averine toward the door.

Later that night in their living quarters, Lonan was beating on a punching bag. He threw a few punches and then some kicks. He hit it so hard that the bag looked as though it would tear from the ceiling. Their home was modest. They didn't need a lot of space because it was just the two of them. They had talked about having children, but Lonan was somewhat reluctant, while Averine was beginning to apply some pressure. Most of their living area was dedicated to study. They each had large desks with multiple computer screens and walls lined with books.

Lonan had several prototype models of projects he was working on at his station. The rest of the home was made up of a kitchen, an area to eat, and a small bedroom. Because their quarters were in the center of the mountain and not along the side, they didn't have any windows. But they did have a solar distributor light in the center of the living area that pulled in light from outside during the day. It was a cozy little area that they kept neat and clean. Averine's side of the study area was a little cleaner than Lonan's.

She had just finished explaining everything from the meeting. The intensity with which Lonan was hitting and kicking the bag showed his level of frustration.

"You know how I feel about these rescue missions. I don't know why you, my idiot brother, and the counsel have to get involved with other planets," he said as he continued to hit the bag.

"How can you just stand by and let them suffer? It's not just men; they take women and children too. How can you not care?" she asked as she leaned against the wall of their little workout corner.

"I do care! You know that. But—"

"But what?"

"But what good is one little rescue mission? Do you know how big this new Nemaron army must be? If they took over Tarnus, then they could crush us," he said as he landed a particularly hard punch. "It's pointless. Just leave them alone, and they'll leave us alone. What good can our little planet do against such a massive force?"

"Some! We can do *some* good," she said as she stepped toward him. "We have to do what's right. Even just a little help is better than nothing."

As she walked closer to Lonan, he stopped punching and turned his attention to her.

"I still think that it's unnecessary, reckless, and foolish, and I don't want you to go."

"Well, I'm going," she quickly replied.

"Well, I'm not!" he fired back.

"I didn't ask you to," she said as she softened her tone a little.

He punched the bag one more time, paused, and then asked, "Is my brother going?"

"Yes."

"Idiot! He and I are going to have a talk." Lonan paused and thought for a moment. "You know that I'm not afraid."

"I know that. I never said you were," answered Averine.

"You two are all that I have, and..."

"I know. You're just looking out for me," she said as she reached over and hugged him.

That night as they slept, Lonan slipped into a strange dream. He found himself in an unknown city. Everything around him looked warped. He couldn't make out the place or faces. The air had a reddish-orange haze, and it seemed to swirl around him. He could hear women and children crying and men yelling. He could barely make out massive soldiers that looked like black shadows killing men off in the distance.

Above him, black winged beings flew and circled him. He looked down and saw his wife holding a crying little girl as they hid in a corner. Suddenly one of the winged beings landed in front of them. As it did, it surrounded them with its wings. Then he heard something that turned his stomach and chilled him to his core at the same time. A deep, gravelly voice called out, "Gruuunaaack, Looonnaaan."

Chapter 4

Lonan woke up and sat bolt upright in his bed. He looked over to see his wife still sound asleep beside him. He reached down and felt goose bumps on his arms. He tried to lie down and go back to sleep, but he was so shaken that he had to get up and get something to drink. Instead of going back to bed, he sat down in the living area and tried to process what he had just seen.

The next morning, the main hangar was filled with activity as crewmen finished fueling one of Helion's largest shuttles. It was a very well-equipped ship; at full capacity, it could carry six, large, ground transports. Both sides of the ship had ramps that folded down to allow the crew to drive a transport in one side and out the other. This made it easy for them to be unloaded quickly. The ground transports they were loading for this rescue mission were called AUVs, which stood for "armored utility vehicles."

Lonan and Telgrin had a lot of input in the design, as the AUV had been one of their first projects directly out of the academy. The AUVs were designed to carry large equipment or large numbers of soldiers. They were well armed, with numerous cannons. The suspension changes that Lonan and Telgrin had made were one of the best innovations on these trucks. They modified the suspension in a way that allowed for changes based on clearance and/or terrain.

As the crew loaded the AUVs onto the shuttle, the suspension was compressed and inset to allow for maximum clearance and, therefore, more space inside the shuttle.

Lonan watched as everyone else worked to load the shuttle. He stood with his arms folded as his mind began to ponder two different things at the same time. He was frustrated by the stubbornness of his wife and younger brother. That confused him because, at the same time, a small part of him admired their compassion for the helpless captives.

The second thing that he was thinking about was the design of the shuttle they were loading. They called it "the Mule" because of its heavy lifting capabilities. As designer and lead engineer, Lonan's father had named it. As he stared at the Mule, he could see his father's hands. He remembered coming to this same hangar with his mother as a boy to visit his father as he and many other men built the shuttle. Unfortunately that was one of the last times he saw his parents alive.

As he stood there daydreaming about the past, Lonan didn't notice that his wife had walked up and was standing beside him. She startled him as she asked, "What are you thinking about?"

"Nothing," he said as he jumped a little. "I just sort of dozed off there for a minute. I didn't really sleep that well last night."

"I know; I saw you. Well, we're nearly ready to go. Are you having second thoughts? It looked like you were contemplating coming along on this stupid rescue mission," she said with a grin.

That immediately snapped him out of his daydream as he shot back, "No, I still think it's reckless, and I'm staying here in protest. Are you going to change your mind about this stupid rescue mission?"

"No," she said with a grin, which made him even more annoyed. Then she grabbed him, hugged and kissed him, and said, "I'll see you in three days. Behave yourself." With that, she turned and walked toward the ship.

"Don't do anything stupid."

"I won't."

"And tell my brother I want to talk to him," he said as she made her way up the loading ramp.

Moments later, Lonan's communicator signaled a call. He unclipped it from his shoulder and put it to his ear. "Where are you?"

"I'm here on the ship," said his brother from the other end of the communicator. "Look up at the cockpit."

There in the window of the cockpit sat Sevran, waving.

"Get down here. I want to talk to you."

"Can't we talk over the com?"

"No. Get down here."

Seconds later, Sevran walked up to Lonan where he stood at the edge of the hangar.

"What?"

"I know I can't talk you out of going."

"That's right."

"You're going to look after my wife, right?"

"That's right."

"You know I don't approve of these missions?"

"No? I don't think you've ever mentioned that," Sevran said with a grin. "We've done so many of these missions without any problems, why are you so worried about this one?"

"I'm not worried. Listen, just be careful."

"Of course; we'll be back in no time," answered Sevran as he turned and ran back to the shuttle.

The last of the soldiers were getting on board as the final cargo-bay door shut. He looked up at the cockpit and saw his wife sitting in the copilot seat. She kissed her hand and put it to the glass. Lonan just smiled and waved as she got up and went back to her seat in the cargo bay. A second later, Telgrin sat down in the copilot seat and also kissed his hand and put it to the glass. Lonan walked away and shook his head. "We need to get him a girlfriend."

Lonan walked to the outer edge of the hangar as the shuttle rolled its way out the door. Once outside, the engines fired up, and the shuttle gradually lifted off the ground.

Kilgron rolled to the hangar door and stood beside Lonan as the shuttle reached the outer atmosphere, where it fired its main thrusters and rocketed into space. His father-in-law turned to him and said, "Don't worry; they'll be fine. Despite his unorthodox methods, your brother has become a great leader, and your wife is one of our best combat medics."

With that, Kilgron turned his two-wheeled transport and rolled back inside.

"Are you telling me that you don't worry about sending your only daughter on these missions?"

Kilgron stopped. With his back still to Lonan, he bowed his head a little and paused while he chose his words. "She is a grown woman, and she can make her own decisions. Her compassion and selflessness never cease to amaze me. She is so much like her mother. But, at the same time, it eats me up inside that I can't go with her. But serving our people has taken its toll on my body. I would be of no help and would only endanger the mission." Kilgron turned to face Lonan, who was still gazing out the hangar door. "You, on the other hand, have no excuse."

Lonan spun around to face Kilgron. His blood boiled, and he clenched his jaw. Through his teeth he answered, "If I participate, I'll be agreeing with the ludicrous decision made by you and the counsel to plan such a mission. If I did so, I'd only be encouraging your foolishness."

"Foolishness? We're doing what we think is wisest for our people."

"Wisest? That wisdom didn't help my parents."

Kilgron's voice got very serious and deep as he said, "I suggest that you choose your words carefully before you say something that you'll regret."

They both stared at each other for a moment until Kilgron turned and continued on into the hangar.

Lonan stayed at the door, watching his family as they left the planet's outer atmosphere. Max walked over and sat down next to him. The dog looked up into sky at the shuttle and then turned and looked up at Lonan.

"What? I couldn't talk them out of it."

The dog looked back at the shuttle and then got up and walked back in through the hangar door.

"Stupid dog. What does he know?" Lonan said as he watched his wife disappear from view.

Early the next day, the rescue team aboard the Mule gathered in the front end of the cargo bay for a pre-mission briefing. Sevran entered from the cockpit and said, "Gather around, everybody. We'll be touching down soon. Telgrin, get the maps on screen."

Sevran was, at times, crazy and reckless with himself, but when it came to the safety of those he was leading on a mission, he was deadly serious.

Telgrin punched some keys on his computer, and a three-dimensional holographic image of the camp was projected above the meeting table. The computer also showed an image of their ship landing in the outlying areas.

"OK, here's our objective. The slave camp is located ten kilometers out from our landing site. That distance should keep us well outside their sensors."

"Ten kilometers?" asked one of the soldiers.

"Yes, it's farther than normal. We're going to be extra cautious on this mission. We've mapped out the quickest path, and our vehicles shouldn't have any trouble with the terrain. Does anybody have any questions?" asked Sevran as he looked around.

Suddenly a voice came over the intercom: "Yeah, do you have anyone with any intelligence running this mission? My guess is that you don't, so why don't you let me take over?"

Sevran and Averine looked out the window to see Lonan's fighter flying alongside them.

"It's about time you showed up. And no, you can't be in charge," Sevran answered. He then turned to the soldiers and continued. "The rest of you, get to your stations. We're nearing the planet."

Averine stayed at the window and said, "Thanks for coming."

"Yeah, OK. Let's just get this done and get back home."

"I love you," said Averine.

"Yeah, I know."

Moments later, the shuttle approached the dark side of the planet Tarnus. It was night on this portion of the planet, but the moonlight shone so bright that the pilot could easily see the clearing they had picked as their landing site. As the pilot put the shuttle down quietly, they could see the silhouette of the disserted capital city several kilometers off in the distance.

Lonan landed his fighter alongside the Mule. The cargo-bay doors opened as the ramps folded down, and the AUVs and motorcycles immediately began to roll out. Without touching the ramp, Sevran launched himself and his motorcycle as he jumped out of one of the cargo-bay doors.

Lonan pulled his motorcycle from a small hatch that opened on the bottom side of his fighter. He then strapped on his helmet, mounted his bike, and rode over to join the group. All of the soldiers were wearing their full gear. The ones mounted on the motorcycles wore lightweight and flexible body armor. Their communication equipment was automated and located in their helmets. Because the mission was a nighttime operation, they all wore black uniforms, and the motorcycles and AUVs had been converted to black camouflage.

All four of the AUVs had unloaded and were waiting beside the shuttle in the clearing. Averine was in the copilot seat of AUV number two, and Telgrin was monitoring all systems from a mobile command center in AUV number one. As he settled into his seat, he said, "Communications check. Everyone report in."

Meanwhile, ten kilometers away sat the Helienders' objective. The outermost slave camp lay at the base of a mountain range. Across a wide, flat plain lay the ruins of what had been the capital city. They had picked this camp because it was the least heavily guarded and because of its location. They thought that it would be the easiest to slip in and out of without being noticed.

The camp was made up of hundreds of tents surrounded by a three-meter-tall electrified metal fence with razor-sharp wire along the top. On the far end of the camp was the mine shaft the intruders had dug with their drill shuttles. The shaft was outfitted with numerous lift-and-pulley systems for lowering workers and equipment and removing precious metals—the elements and gases that they were stripping from the planet's core.

The inhabitants that had been taken captive were forced to work in these mines as slave labor. They slept in the tents for a maximum of five hours a day. The rest of their day was spent working under terrible conditions in the mines. Many of them didn't live very long.

Heavily armed soldiers patrolled the camp. They were Nemaron soldiers and were not the superpowered Leviathans that had taken over the planet. They were a mixture of mercenaries and hired guns that were functioning as prison guards.

Inside the tents, the slaves slept in cramped bunks. They were all thin, weak, and filthy. Their clothes had been reduced to rags by the grueling labor. In one of the tents, a young family was fortunate enough to have been able to stay together while they were loaded into the transports. The three of them slept on one bunk together. The mother and five-year-old daughter rested there as the father stumbled into the tent and nearly collapsed with exhaustion. The man's wife tried to comfort him as she stroked his matted dirty hair and asked, "How are you?"

"I can't feel a thing. I'm too exhausted," said the husband with his face buried in his makeshift pillow.

"Daddy, when can we go home?" whimpered his daughter, who was playing with what was left of a rag doll she had found.

This broke the man's heart as he looked up and shared a hopeless glance with his wife. They both knew that they had no chance of ever leaving the camp alive.

"Soon, sweetheart, soon," said the desperate father as he tried to hide a tear.

Back at the landing site, all of the AUVs and motorcycles had been unloaded. The shuttle ramps and cargo-bay doors closed as the pilot radioed to the AUVs: "You're all clear. Our sensors show no activity along your path to the camp. We'll be waiting for you here. Be safe."

"Roger that," replied Sevran. "Scouts, roll out."

All of the motorcycle soldiers took off down the path as the AUVs followed behind them in single file. None of the vehicles used any type of light. The mission had to remain completely covert, so they used a form of night vision that was built into their helmets and the cockpit of the AUVs.

The path that they followed took them down through a deeply wooded valley. The vegetation on this part of the planet was heavy in the form of tall, thick trees. The terrain was covered with deep cliffs and ravines. The trees blocked out most of the moon's light, so they were completely dependent on the night vision.

From inside the driver's helmets, the path was completely illuminated, with a blue tint. They also had an automated targeting system that picked up and highlighted all living things moving along the sides of the path. A three-dimensional view of the land and layout of the hills could also be seen inside their helmets.

"Telgrin, your targeting system seems to be working well," said Lonan.

Sevran added, "Telgrin finally engineered something that works."

Telgrin, who sat finishing final preparations at his workstation in AUV number one, said, "Very funny! How about I shut yours off?"

Averine could overhear the conversation through the com link. As she finished packing medical equipment in her backpack, she said, "Could you little boys stop the chatter, and focus?"

"You're right. I'm just getting that pre-mission adrenaline rush." As Sevran said this, he rode slightly off the trail and jumped a twenty-meter gap, laying the bike a little sideways in the air as he did.

"What are you doing? You need to stay tactical. We're here to complete a mission, not screw around," scolded Lonan.

"I'm just getting a feel for the terrain, big bro. Don't worry; I've got everything under control."

Meanwhile, at the far end of the slave camp, an elevator platform rose out of the mine shaft. On it were twenty slaves looking like they were ready to die. When the platform came to a stop, they shuffled forward onto the ground as they made their way back to the tents.

The soldiers around them harassed and corralled them like livestock. A few of the slaves stumbled and fell to the ground. When they did, they were beaten and dragged back to their feet.

One of the Nemaron soldiers taunted, saying, "Come on, you lazy weaklings. Get back to your little cages. It's your fault we're late. If you weren't so useless, we'd have been out of those mines hours ago." As he said this, he shoved them with the butt of his rifle.

Just then one of the slave women fell face-first onto the dirt. Another soldier walked over and kicked her in the side and tried to pull her to her feet. "Get up, woman!" he yelled, but she was dead. He turned to his commanding officer and said, "This one's not making it back to her bunk tonight."

"That's too bad. But she will make it to breakfast in the morning," said the officer, and they both laughed. "Take her to the mess hall."

Another soldier came over, and they each grabbed an arm and dragged her lifeless body out of formation.

Just then Devakin and five of his Leviathans appeared. "What's going on here? You're late!" he barked at the Nemaron soldiers, who snapped to attention.

The ones dragging the dead woman let the body hit the ground.

"We had some problems in the mines today, sir. A group got trapped in a cave-in. We thought that we'd just leave them, but command said that we needed the shaft. So we used the second group to dig them out," reported the Nemaron officer as he stood at attention.

"Get them back to their tents now! We don't want any activity out here tonight. My soldiers are preparing to secure the camp," ordered Devakin.

"Yes, sir," answered the officer as they went back to pushing and shoving the slaves to their tents.

Devakin turned his head back and forth as he scanned the camp. He took in a deep breath through his nose as if he had smelled something on the air. He then slowly exhaled, which sounded far more animal than human.

Chapter 5

The ten motorcycles continued down the forest trail. They rode a kilometer out in front of the AUVs as they scouted the terrain and made sure the way was clear for the heavier trucks. After carefully weaving their way through the trails, they came to a clearing on the side of the hill. From there they could look down over the valley below and see the camp, which lay another two kilometers off in the distance.

The Helion soldiers came to a stop and spread their motorcycles out across the clearing. From this distance, they could see the camp's massive electrified fence. They could also see the tall red probes evenly spaced across the entire area. They were identical to the ones that Nemaron had spread across the capital city as they started their initial attack. Their red light pulsated to a near constant glare and lit up the camp like torches from hell.

Sevran scanned the area and called back to the rest of the team. "AUV number one, we're at the first checkpoint. Do you see us?"

Telgrin received the transmission, but it was interrupted by the sound of an alarm from his computer. At his command center, his holographic image automatically zoomed into the area near the mine shaft.

"Yeah, we see you, but—hold up. We have a problem. There's activity at the far end of the camp near the entrance to the mine."

The motorcycle scouts lifted the visors on their helmets as they turned on the holographic image projected from the console at the base of their handlebars. The image showed the mouth of the mine and the slaves running toward their tents. Then it showed the five Leviathan, led by Devakin. The computer measured the images and analyzed the soldiers. It searched its database for information on the men but reported, "Subjects unknown."

"Sevran, do you see what I see?" asked Telgrin.

"Is that who we think it is?"

"I'm afraid so. What do you want to do?"

"We're not leaving here without saving some of these people. Launch the probes," ordered Sevran.

"Wait, what are you doing?" interjected Lonan. "If those are the Leviathan we've heard about, we should abort the mission."

"Don't worry; we'll get in and get out before they know we were here."

"Are you sure?" asked Lonan.

"Yes. Besides, part of our mission is to get a closer look at these guys."

"What? You're joking, right?" asked Lonan.

As AUV number one raced along the path, three small robotic probes were launched from a hatch that opened on its top. In midair, their own small engines fired up, and they flew to locations spaced evenly over the closest end of the camp. They each slowed down and hovered just centimeters above the tops of the tents. Once activated, the probes emitted sound waves from small hatches that opened on their bottom sides.

"OK, probes are in place. I should be able to use them to also collect some readings on these Leviathan," said Telgrin.

Inside one of the tents, an old man shuffled along as he passed the young family. The little girl turned to her father as she stroked the half missing hair of her doll.

"Daddy, can you play dolls with me?"

"Sweetheart, Daddy would love to, but I'm so tired I really must rest."

As they spoke the sound waves entered the tent. They were of such a pitch that they went unnoticed by everyone. As they reached the old man's ears, he immediately fell asleep and fell to the ground. The young man and his family looked over and assumed that he had died, which was not uncommon in the camps. Seconds later, the sound waves hit them as well, and they too fell fast asleep. One by one, so did the rest of the slaves throughout the camp. Outside the tents, the Nemaron soldiers patrolled. As the waves hit them, they too fell to the ground.

The four AUVs pulled into the clearing where Lonan, Sevran, and the other motorcycle riders had been waiting. Now that the AUVs had arrived, Sevran turned to his soldiers and said, "Penetration team, move out."

Four of the motorcycle riders took off down the path toward the camp. Moments later they had reached the edge of the fence. It was made of thick intertwined metal straps. The fence glowed with a bluish haze and hummed due to the high voltage passing through it. They got off their bikes and immediately went to work unloading equipment they would need to cut through the fence.

After a few minutes that seemed like an eternity, Sevran received a transmission: "Perimeter is penetrated. We're all clear."

"OK, good work. Everybody roll out."

Sevran and Lonan led the way down the trail as the other motorcycles and AUVs followed behind.

Near the center of the camp, one of the Nemaron soldiers laid on the ground after being knocked out by the sound waves. His legs stuck out into the path from behind one of the tents. Just then, one of the Leviathan soldiers walked by while on patrol. Unfortunately they were not affected by the Helion probes. Whatever strange power they had made them immune. Fortunately the Leviathan didn't see the soldier's legs or the probe hovering above the tent.

Back at the penetration point of the fence, the four Helion soldiers were just getting back onto their bikes as the rest of the rescue team arrived. They had cut a large section of the fence out and had done it in a way that redirected all the current through large cables running parallel to and above the razor wire. Doing so had killed the power in that section of fence and made it safe for them to cut through and remove it. The motorcycles passed through first, and as they did, they spread out evenly to create a perimeter and secure their end of the camp. While they rolled in, Sevran whispered into his com, "All bikes report in when you're in position."

As they pulled into position, they turned their motorcycles perpendicular so that the broad side was facing the far end of the camp where the Leviathan had been spotted. As they dismounted, they pulled down stabilizer bars from the frame, which made the bikes stand up straight. They pushed a button on the console, which caused a holographic shield to form at the top of the bike that extended down to the ground and covered the side facing the enemy.

The shield had a metallic quality that changed and reflected the scenery behind the bike. As it did, it filtered out the image of the solider standing behind it. This, in effect, made the bike and the solider invisible. They then pulled out their rifles, which had been attached to the side of the bike.

They knelt behind the cover of the shield and took aim on the far end of the camp. This holographic shield was a feature that Lonan had designed. It allowed the soldiers to take a defensive position out in the open by utilizing electronic and holographic camouflage. They could also use the armor of the bike itself to help shield them from enemy fire.

One at a time, they quietly reported in once they were in position and behind cover. Lonan and three other soldiers had a slightly different defensive setup. They didn't use standard-issue rifles but fully automatic guns that were so large they had to be mounted on the back side of the seat of the bike. This gun was formed from two double-barrel guns, one from each side, that telescoped up and locked together to create one formidable weapon.

The AUVs pulled into the camp and parked outward, facing the fence. The back hatches opened, and the rescue soldiers ran down the ramps. Averine led the group from her AUV, and they quickly and quietly filed into the tents. Inside they immediately went to work loading the sleeping captives onto retractable hovering stretchers they unloaded from their packs. They then pushed the stretchers outside to waiting soldiers, who then shoved them in the direction of the AUVs. They were equipped with a low-power steering system and homing beacon that drew them back to the AUV. From there, more waiting soldiers would push them up into the truck, unload the sleepers, and shove the empty stretcher back to the tents.

Part of the genius of this design was the fact that they didn't have propulsion systems; therefore, they didn't make any noise. This made them perfect for these types of covert operations. Telgrin had designed and built these stretchers, and he was always tweaking them and trying to make improvements.

Back at the defensive perimeter, all was quiet while the other soldiers worked franticly to load sleeping captives. Suddenly Lonan saw something. About forty meters out, a very large Leviathan stepped into view. He turned and looked in Lonan's direction but saw nothing due to the shield. He turned to walk away but then paused. He turned back and started walking toward Lonan. Lonan whispered into his com as he tightened the grip on his weapon. "Look out. I think we have a problem."

Just then a shadow flashed across the path and took out the Leviathan.

From inside AUV number one, Telgrin monitored all the activity. "Wow! What was that?" he asked as he saw the Leviathan disappear from his monitors.

Lonan whispered, "Telgrin, did you see that? What's going on? Where is he?"

Telgrin radioed back, "That Leviathan just disappeared. I can't find him anywhere."

In the center of the camp, Lonan continued to scan back and forth as he called to his brother: "Sevran, I just lost visual on one of those Leviathans. He literally just disappeared."

"I know, I heard. Telgrin, keep looking."

Back in the command center in AUV number one, Telgrin franticly punched keys and scanned monitors as well as the holographic display. "He's nowhere to be seen. I'm checking everywhere. Sevran, I'm getting a little nervous about this."

From his end of the defense line, Sevran knelt beside his bike and scanned back and forth with the scope of his rifle, searching for any sign of enemy soldiers. He radioed Averine: "What's your status on the evacuation? We might need to cut this short."

Inside one of the tents, Averine worked franticly to load slaves on the floating stretchers as she quickly checked vital signs. "We're at 75 percent capacity. Give us just a couple more minutes. I don't want to waste any space on this trip."

Back at the front line, Sevran replied, "Your team needs to double-time it. We need to get out of here soon! I've got a feeling that something strange is going on. I don't think this is the time to gather intelligence on the Leviathan soldiers."

"But we need to find out more about these guys."

"What do you want us to do? Sit down and have a drink with one of them?" asked Lonan as he scanned for enemy soldiers.

The young family was nearly all to safety. Mom and Dad were in AUV number two, and the little girl was on a stretcher and had just been pushed out of the tent to a waiting Helion soldier. Suddenly a screeching alarm sounded from the far end of the camp. Seconds later there was a whistling sound.

"Incoming!" shouted Telgrin.

With no time to respond, a missile landed just behind Sevran. The blast killed everyone in the surrounding tents, as well as five of the Helion soldiers. The compression of the blast knocked Sevran off his feet. It also sent the little girl rolling off the stretcher. She lay partly covered by a tent flap, still asleep and nearly impossible to see.

As Sevran crawled to his feet and picked up his rifle, he yelled, "Evacuate now! Rescue personnel, get back to your AUV! All bike units, hold your positions to provide cover!"

The rest of the rescue soldiers grabbed the last of the slaves and took them to the AUVS.

On the far end of the camp, the Nemaron soldiers opened fire as they ran toward the Helion front line. Sevran and his soldiers returned fire while still behind the cover of their motorcycles. Lonan released a wave of rounds with his massive gun and took out five enemy soldiers in one pass.

From inside his AUV, Telgrin yelled, "Gunners, return fire!"

Two soldiers crawled into the gun turrets mounted on top of the AUVs. They fired missiles on the far end of the camp, taking out large numbers of enemy soldiers and one of the enemy cannons.

There were more, however, that continued to rain down missiles as the rescue team finished loading. One of the Nemaron missiles took out two of the Helion motorcycle soldiers.

"Hold your position!" Lonan yelled.

Telgrin punched some keys in his command center and said, "Let's make another door." Two guns lowered from compartments on the bottom side of his AUV. They fired four small rockets that hit the fence, which destroyed a section large enough for all the AUVs to drive out. At the same time the last of the soldiers entered the AUVs, they closed the back doors.

Telgrin turned to another section of his command center and punched some keys as he said, "Everyone's loaded up. It's time for a little off road."

The AUV's suspension started to change. The tires slid outward as the control arms extended. At the same time, the tires also expanded, as if more air were being pumped into them. This caused the treads of the tires to also extend. The body of the AUV elevated, and its ground clearance more than doubled. The end result was an AUV that looked like it could crawl over anything.

Telgrin called out to all the AUV drivers: "Suspension conversion complete! Let's go!"

The other AUVs had also just completed the same transformation. They threw dirt as the tires spun and headed toward the opening Telgrin had blown in the fence.

No one had noticed the little girl lying on the ground and half covered by a tent flap. Her breath gently moved the hair draped across her face. At the front line, the Helion soldiers were still holding off the enemy while the AUVs continued to launch missiles as they sped out of the camp and into the wilderness.

"Keep firing! We have to give them a head start!" shouted Sevran as he squeezed off a group of rounds.

Suddenly, what looked like streaking black shadows took out one of the Helion soldiers in the center of their line of defense. It was two Leviathan that moved so fast they could hardly be seen. The solider they hit flew backward thirty yards, as did his motorcycle. The impact didn't slow them down. The Leviathan continued on through and followed the AUVs through the fence.

The rest of the rescue team moved very quickly up the path and over the rough terrain. Averine stood in the back, trying to strap down the last of the rescued slaves while something caught her attention outside. In the bright moonlight she could see a cloaked man riding a very fast horse along the right side of her AUV. He was riding on a path that ran parallel to theirs. She squinted to try to get a better look as the trees that separated the two roads flew across her view. As she leaned into the window, the man looked back at her. Under his hood, she saw two bright-white eyes.

"Look out. We have someone coming up on our right side, twenty meters out," she warned the driver.

She crawled up to the cockpit and looked down at the monitor on the center console. She zoomed into the area where the man should have been displayed, but nothing appeared, only the road. She looked back out the window and saw him again.

"He's on a horse. Isn't that a little low-tech for Nemaron?"

"A horse? You mean a big animal with four legs horse?" asked the driver.

"We must have a glitch in the sensors, because they're not picking him up," She said as she looked down at the monitor, which showed nothing but vegetation outside the AUV.

The driver was trying to manage the rough terrain but looked quickly out the window. "Are you sure? I don't see anything."

She looked at the driver for a second and then turned back to the window to find that the horseman was gone. "You can't see… What? Now he's gone."

Just then they heard a loud thud as something very heavy landed on top of the AUV.

They raced along the path as they drove toward their extraction point. Averine's AUV was the last in line as she followed Telgrin in number one. One of the Leviathan had landed on top of the truck. He gripped the machine tightly as they swerved back and forth, trying to throw him off. With one free hand, he pulled his rifle from a holster mounted on his back. With it, he shot numerous rounds into a seam in the metal body of the roof. After weakening, it he started punching it with superhuman speed and strength. Within seconds, he had punched a hole through the roof and begun to tear his way inside.

"Lonan, we need some help up here. They're tearing into our AUV," called Averine.

"I'm on my way," replied Lonan as he squeezed off a few last rounds, packed up his gun, and took off out of the camp.

Inside AUV number one, Telgrin jumped out of the seat at his command station and crawled up into the gun turret as he cried, "Oh no! Nobody messes with my equipment!"

He turned the turret and took aim at the Leviathan tearing open Averine's AUV. Telgrin fired a missile that hit him directly in the chest. The blast was huge, and it sent him flying backward. Amazingly the missile had not killed him, and he caught himself just seconds before he rolled off the back side of the AUV.

Back at the front line, seven soldiers remained as they tried desperately to hold off the Nemaron forces.

Finally Sevran called out, "All bike units evacuate now!"

Immediately they mounted their bikes and took off to follow the AUVs. Some of them continued to fire over their shoulders as they sped out of the camp. On the way out, two more were killed as a missile landed between them.

Sevran mounted up and moved to another position closer to the hole in the fence and, from there, continued to lay down cover fire for his men.

The Leviathan hanging off the back side of Averine's AUV climbed his way back to the front. Just as he did, another Leviathan ran at a tremendous speed and jumped on to number one. He immediately began the tear apart the gun turret as the first soldier went back to the hole that he had started before.

Inside AUV number one, Telgrin shouted, "No! No! No! Get off my machinery! Number three, get this guy off me! Sevran, get your guys up here!"

The turret of AUV number three turned and fired at the Leviathan on number two. Just before impact, the Leviathan tore off the metal top of the turret and used it as a shield to deflect the missile.

Lonan was catching up with the AUVs as he quickly moved through a trail that ran parallel to their road but was lower on their right side.

Once he was within twenty meters, he called out, "Everybody, hold your fire! I'm going in!"

He accelerated as he approached a smooth elevated section of the bank that separated the two paths. He hit this section and launched himself up and above the height of the AUVs. As he did, he threw the bike flat and sideways, with the front of the bike now facing back toward the solider on his wife's vehicle.

He timed it perfectly to the point that his back tire was on a direct collision course with the soldier on top of Telgrin's AUV.

He quickly flipped the switch that activated the additional traction feature. Metal spikes extended from the hard rubber knobs of the tires. Inside his helmet, the automated targeting system took aim at the chest of the soldier on Averine's AUV as it zoomed into the exposed area from the previous blast.

"Fire everything!" shouted Lonan.

The bike unloaded hundreds of rounds and two missiles directly into the chest plate of the Leviathan. They hit their mark, and he tumbled off the back side of the vehicle.

A fraction of a second later, Lonan's rear tire struck the face mask of the other Leviathan. When it did, he twisted the throttle, which spun the rear tire. The metal spikes ripped off the Leviathan's face mask, as well as a bloody chunk of flesh. His mutilated face with sunken black eye sockets and pale, withered skin now lay exposed.

Although the face didn't look normal, he did at least appear to be human. The impact spun him around 180 degrees, just in time to receive AUV number three's missile directly in the face. This sent his body flying backward off number one and under the massive wheels of number two.

Lonan landed smoothly on the far side of the trail and then continued along beside the AUVs as they made their way toward the extraction point.

As the four AUVs raced up the trail, the Leviathan, now a twisted mound of armor and flesh, lay in the road. Thirty seconds after they had passed, he began to move again. Gradually he crawled back to his feet. He took a moment to collect himself and then pulled a weapon from a holster on his back and began to run up the trail toward the AUVs.

Chapter 6

From his new position by the hole in the fence, Sevran pulled out a small grenade launcher and sent four final grenades to cover his escape. As he put away the launcher, he looked down at the console on the top of his bike, and it showed the image of the little girl lying on the ground. The computer also showed her vital signs and that her heart was still beating.

Sevran leaned over in surprise to see that she was lying on the ground directly next to him. She was so close that he had nearly hit her.

"What are you doing here, kid?" he asked as he dismounted the bike and reached down to pick her up.

Sevran looked over and saw the Helion soldier that had been rescuing her. He reached out to check the man's pulse and then hung his head in disappointment as he found nothing.

"Don't worry, kid. I'll get you out of here."

He took off his backpack, bumped everything out, and quickly modified it so that she could fit inside. He then carefully strapped her into place and attached her to his back. He mounted his bike and quickly took off through the hole in the fence as a few stray bullets flew past his head.

Back in the center of the camp, some of the Nemaron soldiers were trying to recover and crawl to their feet as the dust settled from Sevran's last group of grenades. Beside one of the men stood a Nemaron probe. The red mist floating within the globe pulsated in unison with the others. As the action of the battle had escalated, the lights grew in their intensity until they reached a constant blaze.

The AUVs continued to race along the road when suddenly twelve Leviathans ran out of the forest and onto the path. Due to their tremendous speed, they closed in quickly. Lonan had moved up to the front to lead the convoy while two of the Helion soldiers followed behind Averine's AUV on their motorcycles to provide cover.

One of them saw a warning on his console, which made him look back over his shoulder. "We've got more company."

The second soldier looked back and said, "Fire rear flares."

Both of the bikes fired rounds that looked like a spray of fireworks. They hit the legs of the Leviathans in the front, which caused them to stumble and fall while the others just ran over them. The ones that fell immediately got up and continued running. They all pulled their rifles from their back holsters and returned fire. Their rounds missed both the motorcycles, but many hit the back side of the AUV.

The first soldier said, "Rear missiles, aim and fire," to which the bike's targeting system responded by firing two missiles from hatches on the back sides of each bike.

The Leviathan were able to jump over and dodge each of these missiles. Amazed, the Helion soldiers tried again.

"Rear missiles, aim and fire."

Once again, the Leviathan dodged everything while they continued to close the gap.

Just then the cloaked horseman that Averine had seen earlier rode down the side of the hill toward the road. As he did, he drew a sword from underneath his cloak. It was ablaze with blue-white bolts of electricity. He pointed it at the pursuing Leviathans, and an enormous bolt of lightning jumped from the tip and struck the ground directly in front of them. The blast was so large that it created a crater and knocked them all off their feet.

The motorcycle soldiers were startled by the blast and turned to see the horseman ride past them as he rode down off the hill and onto the road. While he passed, he turned his head to face them. All that they could see was complete darkness under his hood, except for his two piercing white eyes. His presence and the power of his gaze scared them to the point that they lost control of their motorcycles and nearly collided with one another. The horseman stopped in the center of the road and dismounted as the Helion forces continued on.

The Leviathan had not been killed, but they were severely injured as they stumbled back to their feet. They dusted themselves off while they slowly encircled the horseman. As they did, their wounds began to mystically heal. The blood stopped, and their torn flesh pulled back together.

"Out of our way, horseman," said one of the soldiers with a deep, gravelly voice.

The horseman spoke with a voice like a multitude as he said, "Look at what you have become. You do nothing but kill and destroy."

At the sound of his voice, the Leviathan stepped backward and took defensive battle stances while releasing a deep battle cry in unison. It was as if his voice had triggered something in their minds. They threw aside their rifles and drew swords from their backs.

As they encircled him, one of them said, "You have no place here. This is our territory now."

The horseman laughed slightly and replied, "Come closer, puppets. I have a message for your master."

At that moment, all the Leviathan attacked. The horseman moved like lightning. His speed was far from human and faster than that of the Leviathan. The first of them lunged with a sword thrust but lost his right arm to the horseman's blade. The fact that he had lost his arm didn't affect him, as he jumped back to his feet and rejoined the fight.

The second soldier that attacked had all his blade swings blocked. Quickly he received the horseman's blade in his gut and out through his upper back. Then in one quick motion, the horseman removed his blade, spun, and cut off his head.

The next soldier stepped in to attack as the last one's body hit the ground. The battle continued like this until all the Leviathan lay dead. Throughout the entire fight, the horseman went untouched by any fist or blade. His face remained covered by the shadow of his cloak as it whipped around his body like a shield. Once the last Leviathan's body fell, the horseman sheathed his sword and got back on his horse. He then turned and followed the AUVs.

The four remaining motorcycles and Lonan arrived first at the extraction point. The motorcycle soldiers rode directly into the cargo bay, loaded their bikes, and then ran back out to provide cover. Lonan quickly stowed his bike in the cargo hatch of his fighter. The pilot of the main shuttle fired up the engines as the AUVs rolled into the clearing. As they approached the shuttle, their suspension systems compressed back down to the compact configuration. Once they had finished, they rolled up the ramps and into the shuttle.

Meanwhile, Sevran raced along a section of the road with a deep cavern on his left and a steep cliff face on his right. His computer console signaled an incoming missile, and seconds later, it hit the road in front of him. The blast caused the cliff face to collapse, completely blocking his path. He stopped and surveyed the damage.

"Great! Now what do we do, kid?" The little girl strapped to his back was still completely asleep.

Three kilometers down the road, an armored solider transport carrying Leviathan burst out of the forest and onto the road. As they raced toward him, he made a quick decision and whipped the bike around. He rode back to the left side of the road to the point where the cavern started. As the transport drew closer, they started to fire rounds.

Within seconds, Sevran reached the end of the cavern. There he pulled off the road and traveled through the forest along the other side of the cavern. He continued through the forest, moving at a diagonal, pulling away from the cavern and also from the extraction point.

The transport stopped at the mouth of the path through the forest that Sevran had taken.

"Get him, you worthless slugs!" growled Devakin. "He's trapped. That cavern continues for twenty kilometers."

Ten Leviathan jumped out and ran into the forest while Devakin stayed in the copilot seat. They ran with tremendous speed and agility as they took out their rifles and continued to fire on Sevran and the little girl.

"Take me up to the landslide!" Devakin barked to his driver.

In the cargo bay of the Helion shuttle, Telgrin sat in the copilot seat, preparing for takeoff as he called to Sevran on his com: "Where are you?"

Just then, a blast rocked the shuttle and nearly knocked everyone to the floor. Outside the ship, a crater steamed as an enemy tank crawled to a hilltop eight kilometers away. The ramps and doors finished closing as the engines roared and the shuttle began to take off.

"Everyone, strap yourselves in! We've got to get out of here!" shouted Telgrin

"I'm on my way. I had to stop and pick up someone we missed," said Sevran as he made a very aggressive right turn, which put him on a direct path to drive into the cavern.

"You have a problem. We're in the ship, under fire, and now airborne," said Telgrin.

"No problem. Go to position 2455-21," Sevran said as he glanced down at his console. "I'll meet you there." He yelled back to the little girl, "Hold on, kid."

She snored in his ear as he twisted the throttle and accelerated toward the edge of the cavern.

Back at the landing site, Lonan lifted off in his fighter and took out the enemy tank that had fired on the shuttle. As it sat and smoked, he looked farther over the hill into the valley and saw an entire fleet of surface-to-air tanks rolling toward them. "We need to get out of here now," reported Lonan.

"Roger that," said the pilot as he looked at his monitors and saw the readout of the tanks converging on their position.

In the cargo bay, Telgrin, Averine, and several other soldiers gathered around the holographic display table as they watched Sevran and his direct approach on the cavern.

"He's crazy," said Telgrin.

"You are not jumping that gap. You won't make it," Averine protested.

From the cockpit of his fighter, Lonan watched on his holographic display.

"What do you think you're doing?"

"Sorry, guys, but I don't really feel like talking now. You're all too negative," said Sevran just before he reached up and turned off his com.

At the landslide on the road, Devakin had just finished climbing to the top of the pile of rubble. He stopped to look out over the cavern and could see Sevran far off in the distance. He then started to climb his way down the other side.

In the cargo bay, Averine yelled into her com, "Don't switch me off! Sevran, don't switch me—Idiot! Can he do that?" she turned to Telgrin and asked.

"Yeah, all he has to do is turn off his communications in his helmet…"

"No, I mean can he clear that cavern?" she asked in frustration.

"Oh, uh, let me calculate." He punched some keys on the computer and answered, "Mathematically? It doesn't look like it, but there are too many variables to know for sure. I would need to factor in wind resistance or if he has a tailwind—"

"What does your gut tell you?"

"No. But I've seen him do a lot of things that I can't explain mathematically. He's so annoying," said Telgrin as he shook his head.

Back at the cavern, Sevran crouched down as he accelerated toward a section of the edge that had a very steep rock formation that sloped upward and formed a lip. He looked down at the console as the computer scanned the edge of the cliff and measured the trajectory of different sections. Finally it found a section with a forty-five degree angle and highlighted it on the holographic image.

"That's my spot. Ready all rear missiles."

Rear compartments on his bike opened, and missiles moved out into launch position. Just then the Leviathan following him got close enough to fire some dangerous shots. Sevran ducked to dodge their rounds as he hammered down on the throttle and steered the bike toward the section that the computer was directing him toward.

He drove up the cliff at full throttle, and a second before he reached the edge, he shouted, "Fire all missiles!"

Just as he left the edge of the cliff, all the missiles fired and hit the ground in front of the group of Leviathan who had just run out into the clearing. The blast knocked many of them out, but the rest took aim and fired hundreds of rounds at Sevran as he flew through the air above the immense cavern.

While in midair, he turned the bike sideways, took his right hand off the handlebars, and fired several shots back at the soldiers as their tracer bullets flew by his head. Then he turned the bike back straight just in time to barely clear the cavern.

As he landed, the suspension compressed completely. The landing was so hard that it nearly knocked him off the bike while the little girl still slept on his back.

"That wasn't that hard," he said as he reached up and turned his communications back on. "Did you see that? I don't know why you guys worry so much."

Everyone in the cargo bay of the main shuttle sighed in relief as Lonan came across the radio, "You're a lucky idiot! That's all I have to say!"

"You've got another problem," interrupted Averine. "We have surface-to-air tanks converging on your new extraction point. You're running out of time."

Lonan looked at the monitors in his fighter to find incoming ships off in the distance.

"We have a couple fighters coming in from another base. I'll take care of them. You pick up genius," he said as he turned his fighter to engage the enemy tanks.

He fired and took out the closest three that were in range and were firing on the shuttle. As he did, the pilot of the Mule, which hovered over another canyon, turned the ship and flew toward the new extraction point.

Moments later the shuttle arrived to find Sevran still several kilometers off in the distance and racing toward them. The new location he had picked was a peninsula of elevated land surrounded by deep caverns on all three sides.

"I see you. Don't land; I know we don't have time," said Sevran.

Suddenly a shot was fired from the cover of the dark forest on his right side. It hit the front of his bike and took out his weapons system. Then Devakin ran from the forest at an incredible speed. He could see the shuttle off in the distance, and he ran toward it to cut off Sevran's escape.

"Come down to thirty meters off the cliff, and open one of the doors!" shouted Sevran into his com as he raced toward the end of the peninsula where the main shuttle was beginning to descend.

Meanwhile, on the other end of the cavern, Lonan engaged the two enemy fighters, two against one. They both opened fire as he dodged and flew directly between them and off in the other direction. They both pulled up to follow him. Once he saw that they were beginning to close in, he accelerated to draw them away from the Mule and his team.

The enemy fighters were extremely fast and, in seconds, had caught up to Lonan and were firing on him. He turned on his rear targeting system, and cannons extended down from the bottom side of his fighter. The cannons fired, but the enemies dodged every shot.

Lonan fired again. This time he was able to take out one of the wings of the lead fighter. It didn't explode immediately, but without a wing, it fell to the surface of the planet and crashed into the side of the cavern wall in a tremendous fireball.

Back at the extraction point, Sevran was only one hundred meters away from the edge of the cavern. The shuttle hovered above the edge of the cliff with its largest cargo-bay door open and with the loading ramp down. Devakin raced toward a group of tall trees that sat just below the shuttle on the edge of the cliff.

Sevran accelerated as he drove up a section of the cliff that was nearly straight up and down. It threw him completely vertical into the air, and as he climbed, he drew closer to the open ramp of the cargo bay. His trajectory threw him just high enough to get him over and onto the ramp. He landed on it and quickly rolled into the cargo bay. As he came to a stop, smoke poured from the engine and the now missing front weapon system.

Just then Devakin flew up through the tree and jumped from the highest branch. He was able to jump so high that he grabbed the platform. Averine saw this, ran to the control panel, and quickly closed the door. As it closed, it caught his hand and severed four fingers. That sent him falling back to the planet as he growled in pain. He hit the ground with an impact that would have killed a normal man.

Inside the cargo bay, Sevran and Telgrin walked over to find the fingers lying on the floor. They wrinkled their faces in disgust as Averine put on a rubber glove and picked up the bloody fingers.

"Well, we wanted to get to know them better. I guess that'll happen in the lab," she said as dropped them in the container and closed the lid.

Telgrin reached over and helped Sevran unstrap the little girl from his back. She was still sleeping and uninjured.

Outside Devakin was beginning to crawl to his feet as the shuttle turned on its main engines and flew away.

Many kilometers away above another cavern, Lonan was still locked in an air battle with the last enemy fighter.

"I'm on the ship! Let's go!" radioed Sevran.

"Finally!" said Lonan as he dipped his fighter down into the cavern below.

The fighter followed him in. They rounded a very sharp corner, and as they did, Lonan fired reverse thrusters. This nearly brought him to a complete stop as he hovered around and behind the corner of the cliff.

Seconds later the enemy fighter flew directly past him. He then moved in behind and fired a deadly group of missiles, which instantly destroyed the ship. "I'm on my way," he said as he flew out of the cavern to follow the shuttle.

Far off in the distance, on the other side of the slave camp, the dark silhouette of a winged figure looked out over the valley and watched as the Helion shuttle and fighter took off into space. Then suddenly it jumped into the air and disappeared from sight.

Chapter 7

In the Nemaron command ship, an executive officer entered the living quarters of Maginon. The room was filled with plush comfortable chairs. On the left side of the room, a set of double doors stood closed. The officer walked to center of the room and waited at attention.

The doors slid open, and Maginon walked out while tying the belt of his robe. Inside the room there was a large bed. One of the young women from Tarnus sat on the side of the bed with a blanket wrapped around her and crying. Quickly she got up and ran to a door on the far right side of the room and disappeared.

"You have news for me?" asked Maginon as he poured himself a drink at the bar.

"Yes, sir, we are tracking the menacing group that has been taking workers from the mines."

"Excellent," replied Maginon as he sat down on one of his plush chairs facing a floor-to-ceiling window that looked out into space. "Take them alive. I want to interrogate them myself. Soften them up a bit at the camps first."

"Very well, sir," said the officer as he saluted and then turned and exited the room.

Back on the Mule, Averine examined one of the fingers in a small lab. She cut off a small piece, placed it into a glass test tube, and then loaded it into a machine. As the remaining part of the finger lay on the table, a robotic arm scanned it while Averine turned to a computer screen and waited for results. Just then Sevran and Telgrin entered.

"How are your patients?" asked Averine.

"Everyone is extremely weak and malnourished but stable. What have you found out about these freaks?"

"The computer is showing nothing out of the ordinary. It's a completely human finger, with no DNA modifications," answered Averine with a puzzled look.

"What?" asked Sevran as he walked around the exam table to take a look at the screen. "That can't be right. How can they move the way they do? You saw that guy jump twenty meters into the air. You're sure they're not an alien species?"

"Their DNA is completely human. I'm going to run more tests, but so far I have no biological explanation."

Telgrin added, "I've been going over the data that we collected during the mission. I'm not getting any answers either. I had my equipment scanning them the entire time, and I've got nothing. We were able to pick up their location, so the computer can see them, but I couldn't collect any data on their bodies or vital signs or anything. It's like something was jamming our equipment."

Just then an alarm sounded throughout the ship, which sent them running out of the lab to the cockpit.

"What's going on?" Sevran asked the pilot as they entered the cockpit.

"Look out!" yelled Lonan through the com. "You've got two fighters gaining on you fast. Bank hard to the right, now!"

Two enemy fighters were closing in on the Helion shuttle as it turned a sharp right. The enemy crafts were bigger than the two that Lonan had taken out on Tarnus. These were large, well-armed, deep-space destroyers. They followed the Mule as it tried to evade them.

Lonan dropped into position behind the Nemaron fighters and fired a pair of missiles. He just barely hit the leader, but the blast didn't cause much damage. It was a badly placed shot, and they were heavily armored.

The second enemy fighter peeled off and banked to the left to double back around and attack Lonan. The lead fighter stayed on course and fired a group of missiles at the Mule, whose pilot was trying desperately to outmaneuver the smaller and more agile fighter.

Immediately after the enemy fired, Lonan let loose a wave of missiles and rounds. These hit the mark and destroyed the lead fighter in a tremendous explosion. But the missile the Nemaron fighter had fired continued on and was closing in on the Helion rescue team.

Inside the cockpit of the Mule, another alarm sounded. Telgrin jumped into the copilot seat as the navigator sitting behind the pilot reported, "Sir, that missile is locked onto us and closing fast."

Just then the second enemy fighter moved up into an attack position behind Lonan. It fired several shots. Some hit but didn't cause much damage.

Inside Lonan's cockpit, his alarms sounded, and lights flashed from the damage his fighter had sustained. He took immediate action and banked hard to the left.

The Nemaron missile closing in on the Mule suddenly detonated two hundred meters behind the ship. The explosion caused strange shock waves that passed over the shuttle. It was one of the catalyst missiles. As the shock waves passed over the shuttle, it completely lost power. The engines shut down, and it began to float and tumble helplessly.

Inside the cockpit, the crew sat in darkness except for the dim glow of the emergency lighting. They scrambled around testing all the computers and controls.

"All systems are dead—everything," said Telgrin as he frantically tried to find something that was still working.

As the ship floated quietly through space, it drew near to a small barren moon.

"It looks like we're caught in the gravitational pull of that moon. Switch to manual flaps. We're going to crash-land this thing," said the pilot as he and Telgrin reached down to the floor and removed panels that revealed foot controls.

They both used all their strength to push and pull on the steering system to keep the ship level as it drew nearer to the moon.

From his fighter, Lonan watched as his wife's shuttle tumbled through space.

"Shuttle number one, come in. Anyone on the Mule, can you hear me?"

He waited but only heard static. As he tried to reach someone, the second enemy fighter continued to bombard him with hundreds of rounds. He did the best he could to avoid the enemy fire as he watched the shuttle clumsily coast into the thin atmosphere of the moon.

Telgrin and the pilot continued to struggle with all their strength to keep the nose of the shuttle up as they drew ever closer to the soft gray sand of the barren moon. As they approached the surface, the gravitational pull caused them to pick up speed. With a jarring impact, they hit the surface, and a huge cloud of sand flew hundreds of feet into the atmosphere. They slid along the sand for several kilometers, and the friction caused the wings to break off. Finally the shuttle came to a slow stop, and they all sat back and gave a sigh of relief.

The crew members in the cockpit were collecting themselves and checking their wounds when one of the Helion soldiers ran in. He had blood running down his face from a cut on his forehead.

"Sir, the AUVs still have power. They got banged up badly, but the power cells are fully operable."

Sevran turned to Telgrin and said, "They've been converted over to the hydrocells."

Sevran ran out of the cockpit and into the cargo bay, where he climbed into the nearest AUV. He sat down in the driver's seat and turned on the communications.

"Mule to base, come in."

He heard a woman's voice reply, "Base to Mule, what's your status?"

"Not good. We've crash-landed. They knocked out all our power. The ship is damaged beyond repair. We need an evacuation."

"Are you OK?" asked Lonan as he intercepted the transmission. "How is Averine? Is she OK?"

"She's fine."

From the cockpit of his fighter, Lonan saw a large Nemaron transport flying through space toward the small moon.

"Great! It looks like you have a recovery team on its way to your location. I think they want their slaves back."

One of the Helion soldiers ran into the AUV. "Sir, we've examined the shuttle's fusion cells. They've been completely neutralized. Somehow that shock wave wiped them out entirely."

"Wire the AUV hydrocells to the shuttle's power system," ordered Sevran.

"Yes, sir," replied the solider, who then ran out of the AUV.

Back in the Helion command center, soldiers scrambled as Kilgron called back to the shuttle, "We're getting a rescue team on their way now."

"You can't come here with a standard fusion-powered ship. They'll take you out with whatever they used on us. Hydrocells are the only thing that didn't get shut down by their missile," reported Sevran.

From the cockpit of his shuttle, Lonan added, "But we don't have any shuttles fully converted to hydrocells."

"I'll get the men working on it now. We'll be there as soon as we can," said Kilgron.

"Give them full access to my files! They're going to need my design specs!" shouted back Lonan as he struggled to outmaneuver his attacker.

Not far from the small moon, the second enemy fighter still pursued Lonan. Missiles and smaller rounds flew by his cockpit, just missing him. Off in the distance, he could see the Nemaron ship as it closed in on the shuttle's position.

"Maybe I can take out the recovery shuttle before it gets to you."

"With one small fighter? What are you, crazy?" yelled Sevran.

"Yeah, I'm the crazy one," said Lonan with a sarcastic sigh.

With the enemy fighter still attacking him from behind, Lonan turned his fighter directly toward the recovery ship and opened fire with every weapon he had. The ship's shields absorbed most of the blasts. As he flew past, they fired large cannons that rocked his fighter on impact. While he flew through the blast, his alarm system sounded an intense warning. Lonan pulled off his attack and flew back out into empty space.

On board the recovery ship, one of the Nemaron soldiers turned to his commander and asked, "Sir, do you want us to capture the fighter as well?"

"Tell the fighter to destroy him. We don't need to interrogate one fighter pilot."

The pilot of the second Nemaron fighter received word from the recovery ship and intensified his attack. He had become extremely aggravated by the fact that he couldn't destroy Lonan's fighter and was losing his patience.

Meanwhile on the surface of the moon, the shadow of an unseen being flew through space and landed beside the disabled shuttle. The shadow seemed step through what appeared to be a portal as it walked toward the craft. As it did, it slowly materialized and became visible.

Chapter 8

It was a large muscular, horrific demon. He had enormous black, bat-like wings and charred, wrinkled skin. He wore crude black armor—a chest plate, helmet, and thigh guards—and carried a large sheathed sword on his belt. His eyes burned with a ghostly red haze. As he walked toward the shuttle, he drew his sword, which was encircled in a blazing red flame.

Then, like a gust of wind, an invisible force hit the demon from the side and knocked him off his feet. The demon struggled to collect himself as the cloaked horseman from Tarnus stepped through a portal. The horseman jumped down off his horse, which could now be seen more clearly. It had large wings protected by armor on the front edges, as well as a helmet and chest plate.

The horseman pulled off his cloak to reveal his own wings. He was a massive angel. His wings were covered in thick feathers. His body armor was made of an ancient burnished bronze. His eyes burned bright white. He drew his sword as he stepped in between the demon and the crashed shuttle. His sword was ablaze with bolts of electricity.

As the demon got to his feet, he spoke in a deep raspy voice and growled, "Geldon, I haven't seen you in millennia. You were foolish to allow these humans to come here."

"Mammon, you look as charred as ever. You know how they are. They do as they wish," answered Geldon with a grin.

Just then Mammon threw a surprise sword thrust, which Geldon blocked with his blade as he stepped aside to avoid the attack. He then countered with a strike that deeply cut Mammon's upper thigh. It gushed black blood for a moment and then healed instantly, leaving a deep, brown scar.

Geldon grabbed Mammon and slammed him into the side of the shuttle so hard that it dented the metal of the ship. Inside the cockpit of the shuttle, the crew felt the impact.

"What was that?" asked Averine

"Emergency systems are back on," said the pilot as a few of the computer monitors and dim emergency lights turned on.

Just then another impact rocked the shuttle. They looked outside and saw the enemy recovery shuttle coming in for a landing.

"Oh no, we have company," said the pilot.

"Looks like we don't have much time," said Averine as she sat down at the nearest control panel.

Outside, opposite where Geldon and Mammon battled, the Nemaron recovery shuttle landed. Soldiers immediately poured out of the ship and began cutting a hole in the side of the cargo bay of the Mule.

In the cockpit of the AUV, the computer system struggled on partial power, barely emitting: "Warning. Hull breach. Warning."

Sevran grabbed a headset and spoke into the mouthpiece: "They're breaking through the rear of the cargo bay! Everyone grab whatever weapons we still have, and get down here!"

He fired up the targeting system of the AUV and turned the gun turret to take aim at the side of the ship, where he could now see the enemies' torches cutting though. The remaining Helion soldiers filed into the cargo bay and took aim.

Seconds later the Nemaron soldiers finished cutting the hole. The metal hull of the ship fell to the ground as Leviathan began to file through. Sevran fired a round and took out the first six soldiers while the rest of the Helion soldiers also opened fire.

But then another wave of Leviathan flooded the cargo bay and quickly and easily disarmed the Helion soldiers, taking them captive. Sevran was pulled from the AUV and knocked unconscious with one Leviathan punch to the face.

Outside the shuttle, Geldon and Mammon continued their battle. Their swordplay was so fast that the lightning of Geldon's sword and the flame of Mammon's blade created a blur of light. As their blades collided, sparks and flames flew through the air and fell to the ground. They were nearly perfectly matched in skill.

Mammon, however, was bigger and appeared to be stronger, but that didn't discourage Geldon in any way. He fought with complete confidence and intense determination. With one sword strike, Geldon was able to clear the demon's blade enough so that he landed a powerful kick to the face, sending his opponent flying backward and landing on his neck.

That gave Geldon enough time to jump over the shuttle to the far side, where the Leviathan were filing into the Helion shuttle. In one lightning-fast punch, he sent six of them flying fifteen meters through the air.

Just then, a second demon stepped through a portal and appeared before Geldon. At the same time, Mammon flew over the shuttle and slowly lowered himself to the ground with his massive bat-like wings.

"I told you that you should not have allowed these humans to come here," growled Mammon as he and the second demon walked toward their angelic opponent.

They began to circle him with their sword tips dragging on the ground, leaving a thin trail of flames in the sand. Then simultaneously, the two demons attacked with a fury of sword strikes. Geldon's eyes blazed with intense white light as he fought both demons at the same time. They attacked him from opposite sides. He defended himself, turning back and forth at a speed that was so fast it could only be seen by angelic or demonic eyes.

For several minutes they continued in this battle as Geldon held his ground. From time to time, one of the Leviathan soldiers tried to step in and attack him, but they were quickly sent flying through the air in defeat.

Out in the space surrounding the small moon, Lonan was still locked in a dogfight that he appeared to be losing. In the center of his control panel, he could still see an image from a camera inside the cockpit of the main shuttle.

Then he heard the shuttle's onboard computer system calling out, "Warning. Hull has been breached. Warning. Hull has been breached."

Seconds later, Averine's face appeared on the screen.

"Lonan, are you still there?"

"There you are," he said in relief. "Yeah, I'm here. What's going on down there?"

"They've entered the ship, so I don't have much time."

"Stay where you are; I'm on my way to get you."

"No, don't come. We're outnumbered. Go home, and get help. We'll be OK." She paused and then, in a very serious tone, said, "But even if we don't make it out alive, I want you to know that I love you very much, and I don't want you to be afraid."

"Afraid? I'm not afraid! What are you talking about? I'm coming to get you!" he yelled.

Just then, one of the Leviathan entered the cockpit and grabbed Averine. She punched him in the face twice, but it had no effect. He quickly and easily grabbed her, wrapped her up, and started to carry her out of the cockpit.

As he did, she yelled, "Lonan, go get help! Don't come by yourself!"

Lonan watched helplessly as they dragged her away. "Averine! No! Averine! I'm coming!"

He stared at the monitor in disbelief as she disappeared. Then Devakin entered the picture and stared at Lonan on the monitor. He smiled as he said, "Come and get her. We'll be waiting."

Then he punched the computer, destroying it and ending the transmission. On Lonan's monitor, he could see nothing but a black screen with some white static. He sat silently and didn't seem to notice that his shields were still taking hits from the enemy fighter.

Back on the moon, the Mule had been reduced to rubble, and the Leviathan continued to load the slaves and the Helion soldiers onto their ship. Sevran was just coming to as a particularly large soldier carried him out of the shuttle. Averine was being carried directly behind him, and she kicked and tried to fight her way out of the hands of her captor.

They both looked to the area where the angel and demons were fighting, which was directly beside them and only five or six meters away. They could not see the battle going on. They could see shadows and quick momentary flashes of light from the blades, but they could not actually see the fight.

The movement of the shadows caught their attention, and Averine asked, "Do you see that? What is that?"

"I see something, but don't take my word on anything. My head is still spinning," Sevran said as he blinked and tried to focus his eyes.

Just then the side of the ship dented inward for no apparent reason. They could see nothing there until they caught the faintest hint of a shadow. In reality it was Mammon being slammed into the ship by a perfectly placed punch in the chest. None of the Helion soldiers or slaves could see the angel and demons.

The Leviathan had somehow developed—or been given—the ability to see this spirit world. Averine had been able to see the angel as a cloaked horseman back on Tarnus, but only because he had allowed her to. The Leviathan continued on into their recovery ship. Once they had finished loading all the slaves and Helion soldiers, they closed the loading ramp and took off into space.

As they took off, Geldon and the two demons continued their battle. Geldon had grown very tired but had not lost hope. As his breathing grew heavier, he said, "Two against one. You never did understand the idea of a fair fight, did you?"

The demons laughed as they intensified their attack. Suddenly the second demon caught Geldon off guard. He was able to thrust his blade into Geldon's right shoulder, through the small gap between his chest place and shoulder shield. Geldon cried out in pain as he dropped the sword in his right hand. As it fell, he quickly caught it with his left and then thrust it backward behind him and up underneath the chest plate of the demon. He sank it so deep that it penetrated its heart.

This was a deadly blow, and the demon's body began to slowly dissolve. With his right shoulder badly wounded and his blade stuck underneath the chest plate of the demon, Geldon was wide open for attack.

An instant later, Mammon attacked with a clear swing of his sword that instantly beheaded Geldon. His body fell to the ground and quickly began to dissolve into a combination of dust and a faint mist. The demon's body did the same. Their weapons and armor remained, but their bodies disappeared.

Mammon threw back his head, flung open his wings, and roared in victory. A moment later, a beast stepped through a portal and into sight. It had the appearance of a dragon. It stood on four legs and had enormous bat-like wings similar to those of the demons. Its skin was horribly charred, and some of its flesh was missing, revealing bone and muscle underneath.

Upon a closer look, one could see the slight resemblance of a horse with wings. But its body was now twisted and robbed of its former beauty. It also wore crude deep black armor on its chest, the base of its wings, and across its face as a helmet. Mammon mounted the beast, and they flew off into space.

Meanwhile, Lonan and the Nemaron fighter were still locked in battle. Lonan had used every trick and maneuver he knew to avoid being shot down.

Exhausted and frustrated, the Nemaron pilot said to himself, “If I can’t catch you, maybe I’ll disable you first.”

The enemy then fired a catalyst missile from the tube on the bottom side of his fighter. The missile immediately locked onto Lonan’s ship and followed him wherever he went. The enemy fighter pulled back to stay out of the way, hoping that the missile would do his work for him.

Inside Lonan’s cockpit, his computer repeated, “Warning. Missile lock. Warning. Missile lock.”

“I know, I know!” yelled Lonan as he franticly tried to outmaneuver the missile.

In an attempt to create some distance, Lonan turned on all his main engines and accelerated around to the far side the small moon. The missile followed him and started to drop back.

While Lonan was on the far side of the moon, the enemy pilot's fighter started to malfunction as he hovered there in space. One of Lonan's shots had finally done its job, as the enemy fighter's computer system was beginning to fail.

Steam and sparks were coming from the control panel as the computer reported, "System failure. Syst-em fail—"

The power shut down. The enemy pilot tried franticly to get it working while Lonan came into sight as he rounded the other side of the moon and headed straight for the enemy fighter. As Lonan drew closer, the Nemaron pilot finally restarted his fighter and tried to pull away.

Lonan was quickly closing in on him, with the catalyst missile still in tow. Lonan fired everything he could. The enemy released countermeasures. Many of Lonan's shots were absorbed by them, but one missile made it through and found its mark. The enemy fighter exploded in a tremendous fireball.

Inside Lonan's cockpit, his computer system still warned him of the missile lock. Seconds later the catalyst missile exploded, and the shock waves reached out just far enough to engulf Lonan's fighter. Immediately his ship lost all power, and he tumbled end over end through space.

Off in the distance, Lonan could see the enemy recovery ship that carried his family away in the opposite direction. He worried deeply for his wife and brother. Out of the corner of his eye, he also saw the Mule shuttle lying in pieces on the moon. For a moment, his thoughts drifted to his father but then immediately back to his wife.

Chapter 9

Off in a distant corner of galaxy 55X13 was a barren volcanic planet. Thousands of demons flew around it, patrolling the outer atmosphere. Many of them hovered on their mutilated, winged horses, acting as sentinels on guard. Mammon appeared before the planet as he and his horse stepped through a portal. As he drew near, the demon guards bowed their heads in submission to the higher rank of the passing warrior.

He continued on and flew toward a large crater in the center of a wide valley surrounded by erupting volcanoes. He flew through clouds of fume and ash that spewed from crevasses lining the sides of the volcanoes. The deep red-orange glow of lava covered most of the planet's surface.

Mammon flew toward a crater that rose up from the center of a wide valley. This wasn't the mouth of a volcano. It was clear that the crater had been created by a tremendous impact. It was dark and had only the slightest hint of an orange glow that seemed to come from deep below the surface.

Mammon flew his horse directly into it and dove down into the planet. The walls of the cavern were covered with jagged rock. After diving deeper and deeper, he finally reached the bottom, which lay several kilometers below the surface.

He dismounted his animal once he had reached the floor of what could now be seen as the entrance to a complex system of caves. The caves led in many different directions and had hundreds of demons flying in and out of them. As Mammon approached, the mass of demons parted to allow him through. While he passed, they bowed in submission, to which he responded with a slight nod of his head and a deep grunt.

Mammon reached the entrance to one cave that had two very large demons standing guard. When they saw him coming, they pulled their staffs back to themselves and bowed their heads low as he entered a throne room. On the far left side, there was a cliff that looked over an enormous lake of lava. The chamber was cut into the side of a volcano.

As he entered, Mammon could hear the horrific screams of men being tortured somewhere nearby. In the center of the far wall stood a large stone throne that had been cut out of the rock. Most of it was covered by shadow, but on it, he could see the outline of a dark figure. As he drew closer, he saw a pair of intense red eyes appear from the darkness.

A chill ran up his spine as he said, "My lord, Satan." He bowed low. "I bring news; our pets have recovered some slaves that were lost."

From the shadow came a haunting voice: "*Our* pets?" growled Satan.

"Your pets, my lord," responded Mammon as he cringed in fear and disdain. "They captured the menacing group of humans that has been stealing your slaves, and in the battle, I disposed of one of His servants."

The moment Mammon said, "His," Satan twitched and slipped farther into the shadow, as did Mammon and the rest of the demons.

"The one called Geldon is no more," continued Mammon.

"Fool. You celebrate as if this were a great triumph. I don't care about those worthless humans or subordinate angels. I only care about the mission at hand. Find me the great gate!" Satan growled. His voice shook the cave, and all the demons in the throne room stepped backward.

"Yes, but that's the most fortunate news, my lord," Mammon said as he stepped forward. "We've found the portal to Heaven."

Satan sat forward on his throne but with his face still covered in shadow. "Finally! Send word immediately to gather my legions and finish preparations in the slave compounds. I want more power."

"Yes, my lord," said a small demon as he jumped from the shadow where he had been cowering. Immediately he flew from the chamber.

"Mammon, I want you to personally oversee the conversion of our latest batch of Leviathan. I'll need as many soldiers as possible if I am to break through the great gate."

"Yes, my lord," Mammon said as he bowed low and backed away from the throne. He then turned and flew down into the volcanic crater on the side of the throne room.

Most of the bottom of the cavern was filled with boiling lava. The sides of the cavern were steep walls covered with jagged rock that had thin walkways carved into them. Along these walkways were small caves hollowed into the rock. Crude iron bars blocked the mouths of the caves, and behind them were hundreds of men struggling to escape.

Across the center of the cavern spanned a system of cables and metal walkways that lead out to a large circular arena. On it stood fifteen men. They walked around the arena in nothing but rags. They looked around the cavern in horror and confusion as fifty demons flew around the outside of the arena.

The men had grown weak and emaciated from lack of food and water. The blood and wounds all over their faces and bodies showed that they had already been beaten numerous times.

The demons circling them began to close in. The men could feel the wind generated from the beating of their massive bat-like wings. The sound of their chilling voices penetrated the men's minds as the demons began to yell and curse as they closed in around them.

"You're all going to die!"

"Kill!"

"You're worthless!"

"Kill!"

Chaos erupted as the men huddled in the center of the arena and cowered in fear.

"Kill!"

"You're nothing!"

"Kill him before he kills you!"

"Kill!"

"Everyone you love is dead!"

"Kill!"

"He hates you!"

"Kill!" the demons shouted.

The men were thrown into such terror and confusion that they turned on each other. Like thoughtless animals trapped in a cage, they fought each other as if the men beside them were their captors. Blood flew in all directions as they brutally attacked each other in hand-to-hand combat. With every ounce of their limited strength, they tried to destroy each other. They had lost all control, and the demons continued to scream curses and cheer as the blood was spilled.

"Kill, or you will be killed!"

"Die!"

"You are worthless!"

As the men fought, a blackish blue substance collected in the veins near their ears. It seemed to crawl under their skin like parasitic worms as it moved toward their eyes. The violence and brutality continued to escalate as two of the men fell and were beaten to death. This brought great cheers from the demons, who howled in delight.

Red mist emanated from the arena and grew so thick that it became difficult for the demons to see the battle. They bathed in it and drank deep of the mist as they began to fight each other for more of it.

Mammon hovered above the area and watched with great delight as two more men were strangled to death. After those two fell, he flew down to the side of the arena to where a door led out onto a walkway. This door and walkway ended at a metal staircase that led down to a large cave at the very base of the cavern. Mammon pulled a whip from his belt and cracked it with such immense power that all of the demons jumped back in fear as the men fell to the ground.

"Enough" he growled as he opened the door. "You have graduated to the next level of your training."

Covered in blood and sweat, the men limped out of the arena. As they passed Mammon, he could see that the blackish blood had passed into the whites of their eyes and stained all the skin of their faces. They continued down the metal stairs and into the cave. As they did, they could hear the demons yelling and cursing in the cavern behind them as the next batch of men were corralled into the bloody arena.

They walked deep into the cave and took their places in line behind hundreds of other men who had gone before them. The expressions on their faces were blank but deadly. The sockets of their eyes were filled with the blackish blue color. Their faces were bloody and pale.

As they moved along, they became part of an assembly line. Other blank-faced men stood alongside them and strapped equipment and armor onto their bodies. The first was an ancient-looking piece of metal armor that wrapped around their chests with metal straps. It also had straps that extended up over their shoulders and around their necks. This chest piece encased what looked like a long, upside-down, V-shaped glass vile. It was filled with a pulsating red light, just like the Nemaron globes on Tarnus. Once it was locked into position, sharp metal claws shot out from the side and plunged themselves into the man's flesh. They each cried out in pain, but they also received a jolt of energy that pulsated through their bodies. After the chest plate had attached itself to its host, the man opened his eyes, which were now engulfed by a deep-red flame.

As they continued down the line, more and more man-made armor was added on top of the ancient chest piece. The armor covered nearly every part of their bodies. An additional, larger chest plate was added over the ancient one. The pulsating red light could still be seen through a cut-out section. At the end of the line, they were given a helmet that had a full face mask. They were then handed a rifle as they marched through another cave that led upward toward the surface of the planet.

Meanwhile, in the main control room at Helion, the Helienders finally received a transmission from Lonan.

"Lonan to base. I'm coming in."

A relieved solider radioed back, "Yes, sir, you are clear for landing in the main hangar."

Moments later, soldiers and engineers gathered around as Lonan's shuttle slowly hovered its way in through the hangar door. It was badly damaged and covered by charred blast points. It flew somewhat irregularly as he tried to set it down gently. The engines cut out, and it dropped the last half meter, landing with a crash. Steam poured out of many different areas, and it smelled of burnt and charred electronics.

Lonan climbed down out of the cockpit. As everyone gathered around him, he stood back to take a look at his ship. He frowned and shook his head as he turned and walked away. As he did, he turned to one of the engineers. "Start analyzing the ship. I want to know what they used to shut down our fuel systems. We should be able to reverse engineer the reaction and figure out what happened."

"Yes, sir."

"What's the status of the shuttle conversion?"

"We're approximately 75 percent complete, sir, but we're glad you're back. We really need your help."

"OK, I'll be back in a minute."

"Yes, sir," said the engineer as he turned and went back to the ship. As he did, Kilgron entered the hangar on his two-wheeled transport.

Lonan immediately walked over to meet him. "I told you this was a bad idea! Now look what happened! I'm taking a team as soon as we get a shuttle ready!" he shouted.

"Don't forget to whom you are speaking!" Kilgron shot back.

Lonan ground his teeth as they each took a breath.

"Calm down, and look." Kilgron pointed to a nearby computer monitor. "They're OK. We're monitoring their condition."

The screen showed the captive crew's vital signs and heart rhythms.

"We were all aware of the danger involved in this mission. You need to focus on our present objective, which is to get them home. How did you make it back?"

"I'd equipped my fighter with hydrocells for reserve power. I limped back on that."

"Well done. We're glad you made it out. The team is ready, and we've pin-pointed their location. We just need the shuttle."

"All right, I've got work to do," said Lonan as he turned and walked back toward the shop.

"Lonan..."

Lonan stopped and turned back.

"We'll get them back," Kilgron said.

"I know."

On a distant, lonely planet stood a large building at the base of a mountain. Twelve Nemaron soldiers patrolled the outside of the building. Inside there was a metal rack system that held men, women, and children upside down by their feet. Each of them were connected to an intravenous line, as well as other wires and equipment. They appeared dead, but from time to time, their bodies twitched. The racks hung from the ceilings and suspended the people above large holes built into the floor. At the bottom of these holes were channels of boiling lava. Steam and fumes poured up and over the hundreds of unfortunate souls hanging in the racks.

A group of Leviathan entered the main chamber as they carried Averine, Sevran, and Telgrin. Behind them followed the slaves that the Leviathan had recaptured. They led them through the chamber, down a hall, and into a dimly lit room filled with crude, dirty tables with straps. Two men wearing medical lab coats stood in the room. A man was strapped to one of the tables as they entered. Then two soldiers grabbed him by the arms and dragged his drugged and half-dead body out of the room to the racks.

One of the soldiers in the lab coat grinned as he said, "Next."

Sevran tried to escape as he burst free from the Leviathan soldier that was carrying him. He punched him in the face, but it had no effect. He only laughed and then punched Sevran in the face so hard that it sent him flying backward, and he landed on one of the tables. His nose began to bleed as he moaned.

"That was a great idea," He said to himself as two soldiers grabbed his arms and legs and strapped him to the table.

Back at the Helion base, Lonan and one of the soldiers finished loading the last of their equipment.

"That's it, sir."

"Good, tell the rest of the team we're ready to take off," said Lonan as he climbed into the pilot's chair and turned on the computer in the center console. As he did, the vital signs of his wife and the rest of the team came up. He could see that they were still alive and that their heart rates were elevated.

"Hold on, babe. I'm coming," he said to himself quietly.

Just then, Kilgron's face appeared on another screen.

"Is your team ready?"

"Yes, the men are loading up now."

"I know that you'll bring her back safely."

"Yes, I will. I'm the only hope they have."

"You have the best of our soldiers with you. You will be successful. Failure is not an option."

"I know that."

"Lonan, I know that the situation looks very dark, but I want you to know that I'm sure your parents would be very proud of you and your brother."

"What? Enough. We're wasting time here. Command, we're starting engines and moving out to the hangar."

A woman's voice came across the com: "Roger that, Colt. We are prepping launch rails."

Seconds later the shuttle's engines fired up as it began to roll out of the hangar. This was a newer version of the Mule shuttle they had lost on the small moon. Lonan had designed it by using many of the features that his father had put into his original version. It was similar in appearance and hull design but smaller and not equipped to carry heavy transports, only smaller attack teams. Its smaller size and lighter weight made it much more maneuverable than his father's version. They called this particular ship the Colt.

The modification that they had just finished was a complete replacement of the fuel and propulsion systems. It was no longer fusion powered but equipped with hydrocells. The enemy's catalyst missiles had not destroyed this system, so they decided it would be the safest bet. They had not yet been able to fully analyze Lonan's shuttle to determine exactly what the shock waves of the catalyst missiles had done. They were running out of time and needed to go with the most logical choice.

The hydrocell propulsion system that Lonan had designed was far lighter, which meant that they could travel farther and carry more people with the same amount of fuel.

"How many tests were you able to complete on this new system?" asked one of the copilots as he sat down in the cockpit.

Lonan turned to him with a very serious look on his face and replied, "We're testing it now."

The copilot's eyes widened as he attached his safety harness.

Outside of the hangar, the Colt rolled along until it came to the edge of a cliff. This particular hangar opened onto a wide ledge that was protected by steep cliffs of the mountain on two sides and overlooked a wide valley far below. As they approached the edge of the cliff, the control room radioed, "Launching rails are being deployed now."

"Roger that."

The rocks and vegetation on the side of the ledge began to move to the side as metal rails mechanically elevated from hidden compartments underground. What they revealed was a complete launching system that started near the hangar door, followed down the steep incline of the side of the mountain, across the valley, and halfway up a smaller hill on the opposite side. These were large metal rails that ran the entire distance. Lonan moved the Colt into position as he straddled the rails. Then a massive metal launching pad came up from underneath, attaching itself to the bottom of the shuttle magnetically. Once they were attached, the copilot retracted the landing gear, and the shuttle rested on the launching pad that was now sitting on the rail system.

Lonan radioed to the command center: "We're in position and ready for launch."

"Copy that, Colt. You are go for launch in three, two, one, and go."

The magnetic rails powered up as the launch pad began to glide across the rails. As it did, the shuttle moved over the cliff and quickly accelerated down the side of the steep mountain. Once they reached the bottom and began to move across the open valley, the engines of the Colt fired as it continued to build speed.

Seconds later it reached the far side and began to climb the rails that extended up the hill. When it reached the top of the rails, the launch pad released its magnetic connection to the ship and sent it flying out of the valley and into the sky.

Moments later as they entered the outer atmosphere of the planet, Lonan turned to the copilot and said, "See. No problem."

The copilot raised his eyebrows as he exhaled in relief and whispered to himself, "And they say his brother is the reckless one."

"What was that?" asked Lonan.

"Nothing."

Chapter 10

Early the next day, Lonan and his rescue team approached the small planet where his wife and brother were being held captive.

"We have a clearing to the northwest of the compound," said the copilot.

It was night, and they depended entirely on their computer systems to locate the landing site. Moments later, Lonan maneuvered the shuttle down into position as he landed in the small clearing on the far side of a mountain range.

The compound was nearly three kilometers away, and an outcropping of the mountain stood between the team and it. The twelve Helion soldiers and Lonan filed out of the Colt and gathered at the bottom of the cargo ramp while the copilot stayed to guard the ship.

"OK, let's get in and get out as quickly and quietly as possible. Follow me," said Lonan as they took off running through the thick vegetation, keeping to the shadows and cover of the rough terrain.

Meanwhile in the slave compound, Nemaron soldiers were dragging Averine and the rest of the crew down a hallway. They couldn't walk because they had been drugged. The soldiers locked them in dark, dirty holding cells.

"Tell Maginon they'll be ready for interrogation in fifteen minutes," said one of the Nemaron soldiers.

"Yes, sir," replied a second, who left the cell to relay the message.

Something was happening just outside the landing site where the Colt shuttle and copilot waited. What appeared to be stars or meteors falling from space began to converge beside the landing site. These blazing balls of light slowed and settled to the ground. As the intensity of the light faded, it became obvious that they were angels mounted on armored, winged horses.

There were twelve of them in all. They wore heavy armor very similar to Geldon's. It was worn and dented with scratches and deep cuts. It was obvious that they were seasoned warriors who had lived through some deadly battles. They had noble and serious faces. Their eyes burned with such an intense white light that it looked like it could have burned the flesh from a man's face.

Seconds after they landed, a small force of twelve humans slipped from the shadows. They had blended completely into the darkness, as they were dressed entirely in black, lightweight body armor that covered their entire bodies. They were armed with advanced rifles and long metal blades. Some wore the blades on their backs and others on their hips. The two leaders of this small unit stepped forward. They were called Ahren and Cloin.

One of the angels road forward to meet them while still mounted on his horse. He was called Tekel, and he was the leader of this force of angelic warriors. His armor was heavier than the others. His helmet was the most ornate and had a razor-sharp blade that stood straight up from the forehead.

"This place is well guarded," said Tekel.

His voice was deep and strong. It sounded as if ten men were speaking in unison. His words seemed to nearly shake the ground.

"They're going to need our help. Ten of you, draw the enemies' attention away to the far side of the compound. The other two, stay with them, but remain out of sight. Ahren, take one solider with you, and cover them inside."

Ahren nodded.

"Cloin, lead the rest of your men to the far side. Get their attention, and keep it until the Helion rescue is complete," ordered Tekel.

"Yes, sir. We can do that," Cloin said as she nodded her head.

Cloin was a beautiful young woman. She had long black hair that she wore tightly pulled back. She was one of this team's most gifted and intense warriors. Her focus and precision could not be matched by any of the men. Ahren was her older brother. He was a great leader and strong in body and mind. Together they led this small band of warriors.

"OK, let's move out," ordered Ahren.

Silently they disappeared into the darkness.

Tekel turned to the other angels. "We need to create our own diversion. Follow me."

The strong wings of their horses propelled them into the air as they disappeared into the night sky.

At the compound, Lonan and his unit had just arrived at a small back door. They took cover under the shadow of thick vegetation. He turned to one of his soldiers and said, "Get us in there."

The soldier silently moved out and crossed the small opening without being seen. When he reached the door, he immediately went to work breaking in. He placed a small electronic device on the door's controls, breaking the security code and opening the door in seconds. He drew his rifle and entered the building. He found nothing but a long dark hallway that led to a large glowing chamber at the far end. Seconds later the rest of the unit filed in. Once they were inside, they closed the door and quietly made their way down the hall.

At the end, they came to a large room that served as the main slave chambers. They were disturbed to find men, women, and children hanging upside down in slave racks. Far up in the ceiling, they saw one of the pulsating red globes. It was similar to those on Tarnus; however, this one was ten times bigger. It was lit up with the eerie red light, and it was so intense that it filled the room.

One of the soldiers turned to Lonan and whispered, "What's going on here?"

As Lonan looked around, he answered, "I don't know, but whatever it is, it doesn't look healthy. Let's find our people and get out of here."

Lonan looked down at the small monitor attached to his rifle, which displayed the building layout and dots indicating the location of his family. "This way," he said as he moved out of the cover of the hallway and into the main chamber.

His unit followed him, silently creeping along the outside of the room. As he passed one of the racks, a little girl looked over at him. Her eyes were glazed over with a milky white haze. She reached out her hand for help as he passed. When their eyes locked, Lonan felt every muscle in his body freeze. He stopped and stared in horror at the sight of her in bondage. Seconds later he pulled himself back to reality and continued along the wall.

On the far side of the compound, Cloin led her team as they took cover behind large rocks that stood fifty meters away from the building. She nodded to one of her men, and he pulled out a small, tubular rocket launcher. He took aim at the side of the compound and fired. On impact the rocket blew an enormous hole in the wall. Seconds later the alarm sounded.

Inside, two demons flew around the ceiling. When the wall was suddenly blown out, it grabbed their attention. They immediately flew down to see what had happened. Twenty Leviathan also ran to the door to confront their attackers.

From the outside, Cloin and the other warriors waited under the protection of cover. As the dust and smoke started to settle, the soldiers inside opened fire. Through the layers of smoke came hundreds of tracer rounds.

"I think we got their attention," said Cloin.

Seconds later twenty Leviathan ran through the hole as they fired blindly out into the night. Above them flew twelve demons.

Suddenly the angels appeared in the night sky far above the compound. When the demons saw them, they threw open their enormous wings and roared a deep battle cry. The angels drew their swords, jumped from their horses, and flew down to meet the demons in battle. The demons drew their flaming blades and jumped into the air to attack. A tremendous sword battle began as they collided in midair above the compound.

Down below, the Leviathan continued to fire wildly into the dark. Cloin and the other nine stayed very low and out of site. Then they quickly and carefully took aim with their rifles. Simultaneously they fired tranquilizer darts and hit ten of the Leviathan, who immediately hit the ground, fast asleep. This caught the attention of the other ten. Cloin and her warriors fired again but hit nothing. The Leviathan were now watching for the darts and were able to dodge each of them with their superhuman speed.

Without a spoken command, the unit in black jumped from their positions of cover and ran to attack the ten remaining Leviathan, who immediately opened fire. Every one of their rounds missed. Cloin and her unit were also able to move at superhuman speed, which allowed them to dodge not only their rounds but also their blades and fists.

When the two groups collided, they squared off one on one and engaged in ultrafast hand-to-hand combat. Cloin and her soldiers' eyes began to glow with intense white light as the battle intensified. They pulled their blades and were locked in a battle of

Leviathan speed and power verses the precision and patience of Cloin and her force.

In the air above the compound, Tekel and his angels continued to battle the demons. Their blades collided and rained flames and lightning bolts down over Cloin and her men fighting below. Tekel was more powerful than any of the demons that squared off against him. As they fought, they used not only their blades but also the armor of their wings as shields and at times as weapons.

Two demons attacked Tekel at the same time. As they tried desperately to land a strike, they were unable to withstand the power of Tekel's blade. As he blocked the flaming blade of one demon with his wings, he scorched the other with lightning from the tip of his blade. As the demon reeled in pain, Tekel had time to land a finishing swing of his blade, severing the demon's head. The demon immediately began to dissolve as his armor fell to the ground.

Deep inside the compound, the alarm still sounded as Lonan and his unit crept along the dimly lit hallway and watched as enemy soldiers ran down an intersecting corridor. They jumped back into the shadows as they tried to figure out which of them had triggered the alarm. Just then two Leviathan saw them and ran down the hallway in their direction. As they did, Ahren rolled out of the cover of shadow, fired two darts, knocking out the two enemy soldiers, and rolled back under cover before anyone could see him.

Confused, Lonan and his men looked at the sleeping Leviathan and at each other as they tried to figure out what was going on.

"This place is crazy. Let's get out of here," whispered Lonan to one of his soldiers through his com. They continued down the hallway until they came to a group of cell doors. Lonan peered into the window of one of the doors and called out, "Averine? Are you in there?"

Suddenly a man's face appeared directly in front of him, which caused Lonan to jump backward several feet. The man reached his arm out the window and nearly grasped Lonan's face.

"Help me!" he cried in a raspy voice.

Then Lonan heard his wife in the next cell as she struggled to call out, "Lonan, I'm here."

He stepped over to the next cell and said, "I'm coming, just hang on."

One of the soldiers put a device on the door and blew the lock. They filed in and found the captives lying on a cold wet floor.

"They drugged us. We can hardly walk," said Sevran from the corner.

Lonan ran in and picked up his wife.

"I'm here. Don't worry; I've got you."

"I knew you would find us."

He carried her out of the cell and down the hallway. One of the other soldiers helped Sevran to his feet as he struggled to try to walk. While they left the room, Telgrin, who lay face down on the floor, kicked his leg a little and said, "Hey, don't forget me."

"Yeah, don't forget Telgrin," added Sevran.

With his face mashed to the floor, Telgrin replied, "Thanks, man. I appreciate it."

As they shuffled down the hall, Sevran called to Lonan, "What about all the people we freed from the camp? We've got to get them out."

"We'll get as many as we can, but we don't have much time. This place is crawling with enemy soldiers."

Averine protested: "We can't just leave them here. Did you see what will happen to them?"

Sevran added, "Don't forget the little girl. I think she's in the next cell."

Lonan turned to one of the soldiers. "Open the other cells too, and save as many as you can."

They quickly and quietly crept down the hallway, out into the main chamber, and along the wall to the exit. As they crossed the room, they could see far across to the other side, where the hole had been blown in the wall. Outside they could see the warriors in black fighting the Leviathan. They could barely make them out, but they could see that they moved just as fast as the Leviathan and that they were able to defend themselves against their vicious attacks. Lonan and his men rounded the corner, moved down the hallway, and found the shuttle waiting for them outside.

Lonan set his wife in one of the seats as the other soldiers laid Sevran and the others down in the cargo bay. The Helion soldiers started to walk back out of the shuttle when Lonan asked, "What are you doing?"

"Going back for the rest," answered one of the soldiers.

"We don't have time."

Averine protested: "Lonan, please. Help them." She pulled on his shirtsleeve.

"One last trip, but hurry," he said as he and the soldiers ran down the cargo-bay ramp and back into the building.

As they entered the main chamber, one of the Nemaron soldiers spotted them. Just as he was about to yell to the Leviathan fighting outside, he fell to the ground. Ahren slid back into the shadows without being seen.

Outside, the angels and demons continued their fight. Tekel battled another two demons in the air while some of the angles had landed on the ground and were fighting directly alongside the humans. The demons appeared to have a slight advantage in speed over Tekel's force. But his angels made up the difference in perfection of technique and focus. Their primary goal was to keep the demons occupied as the Helion team completed their rescue.

Lonan looked across the room to try to get a closer look at who the Leviathan were fighting. He knew that they weren't his men. He saw the warriors in black, and he could see Cloin, but he couldn't see the demons or angels that were fighting directly alongside them. His eyes did, however, catch something. He caught a glimpse of shadows moving and the occasional flash of a dim light from the angel's blades.

Then Cloin caught his attention. He saw her hit a Leviathan so hard that he flew backward, hit the wall, and fell unconscious. But then she continued swinging her blade at what appeared to be nothing. Lonan could see nothing but a slight glimpse of a shadow. He shook his head and said, "This place is crazy." He then left the main chamber and continued on down the hall.

What Lonan could not see was that a demon had landed and was now attacking Cloin. She blocked his blade on every swing. Without a trace of fear and with complete focus, she matched the demon's speed and strength and pushed him back until an angel flew down and pulled the demon from her while she engaged yet another Leviathan that had just joined the fight.

Back in the compound, Lonan ran into the second cell. Two Helion soldiers were carrying the last of the sleeping Tarnus captives. Lonan scanned the empty room until something in the far dark corner caught his eye. He stepped closer to get a better look. It was the little girl Sevran had rescued. She was still asleep and had nearly been forgotten again.

"This must be the kid," said Lonan as he scooped her into his arms. One of his soldiers ran in behind him and said, "Looks like she's the last one, sir."

"Good, let's go."

Once outside, Lonan ran up the loading ramp of the Colt. He carefully handed the little girl to his brother and then headed for the cockpit.

"OK, that's it," Lonan said to the copilot as he closed the loading ramp. "Get us out of here—but quietly. Don't draw any attention."

"Yes, sir."

The shuttle lifted off the ground silently and crept away from the compound. Once he had reached a safe distance, Lonan turned on the main thrusters and launched the shuttle into the night sky.

Back on the far side of the compound, the angels continued their battle until the Helion shuttle was gone. When Tekel saw that the Colt was at a safe distance, he pulled a horn form his belt and blew it. Its sound was an immense echo, which caused the demons to cower and cover their ears in pain. All the angels pulled back into the air and mounted their horses. They gathered together as the demons flew toward them in pursuit.

Down below, Ahren ran onto the battlefield from the hole in the wall and threw a small grenade into the air. When it exploded, it emitted such an intense light that the enemy soldiers and demons were blinded for several seconds. By the time they had regained their sight, the warriors in black were gone.

The angels opened their right hands and simultaneously thrust them forward. This created a gust of wind that threw the demons back a hundred meters. The gap gave them enough time to fly off into the darkness of space.

In the Colt, Lonan had settled into the pilot's chair. He looked back into the cargo bay and saw his brother holding the little girl. She was still asleep and a mess.

"Don't worry, kid. We're safe now," he said as he stroked her matted brown hair.

Beside his brother, a medic tended to his wife. She looked into the cockpit at Lonan and mouthed the words, "I love you." He gave her half a smile and turned back to piloting the ship.

Chapter 11

Several hours later, Maginon arrived at the slave compound and walked through the hole that had been blasted in the wall. Ten of his personal armed guards followed him as he surveyed the damage. He tried to restrain himself, but it was obvious that he was angry.

"Where are the captives that I am here to interrogate?" asked Maginon.

"Sir, we had no warning of their attack. They avoided all our sensors," answered the nervous Nemaron soldier.

Maginon began to circle him as he continued to look around the building at the damage that had been done.

"You haven't answered my question. Where are the captives?" he asked again as his voice elevated.

Just then Devakin entered the main chamber from one of the hallways on the far side. As he walked toward them, he interjected, "In the middle of the attack, they seemed to disappear. A few of my men—"

Before Devakin could finish his sentence, Maginon spun around and tried to punch him in the face, but Devakin caught the punch in one hand. He then grabbed Maginon by the throat and lifted him into the air.

"Who do you think you are?"

Maginon began to turn red as he struggled to breathe.

"I have everything under control," said Devakin as he tightened his grip on Maginon's throat.

Devakin then threw Maginon across the room and against a wall. Maginon slid to the floor and gasped for air. His Nemaron soldiers jumped and stood at attention, fearing that they would be next. Maginon choked and writhed in pain as he tried to catch his breath. He looked across the room at Devakin with the deepest hatred in his eyes as he climbed to his feet.

Just then darkness swept over the room as two massive demons flew in through the hole in the wall. They landed beside Maginon and began to circle him while the soldiers slowly stepped away in fear. The first demon mocked, "Look at our little worm showing his muscles. We were here. Are you going to try and punish us as well?"

"Oh, I'm just aquiver with fear," added the second demon.

As they circled him, Maginon stood motionless while deep anger brewed in his eyes.

Just then Mammon flew down and landed just outside the compound. As he walked into the building, the men stepped back even farther. The two demons stopped circling Maginon and stepped back as well. Mammon stepped into the center of the room and looked at Devakin. He narrowed his eyes and let out a low growl. Devakin threw his head back in pain as he fell to his knees.

"All is well! The compound is still functioning at full capacity!" he yelled through his suffering.

Mammon looked up into the ceiling to see the red globe still pulsating.

"Yes, fortunately for you," said Mammon as he turned his gaze to Maginon.

As he turned away, Devakin was released, and he fell to the floor.

Maginon stepped backward as Mammon walked in his direction.

"We have tracked their ship and now have their location," said Mammon as he drew very near to Maginon's face.

Maginon tried not to show any fear as the stench of the demon's foul breath filled his nostrils.

"You will see the captives soon enough."

Back at the Helion base, the rescue team had just arrived. Kilgron, General Crine, and the entire counsel were there to meet them. Lonan brought the Colt in for a landing in the main hangar. Once it came to a stop, thirty soldiers and medics converged on it as the cargo-bay ramp opened. Within seconds, they were unloading the wounded and taking them to the medical bay. Lonan and one of his soldiers carried Averine down the ramp on a stretcher as a female medic examined her. Kilgron quickly went to her side.

"I'm fine. I just feel sick from the drugs."

"I'm so glad you're safe," he said as he grasped her hand. Not shedding a tear, he maintained his extremely tough exterior. However, he could not hide his joy and relief.

"Get everybody to the medical bay," said Lonan as he pushed Averine's stretcher forward. "You can visit her there."

Sevran and Telgrin hobbled off the shuttle as a soldier helped each of them along.

"I feel terrible. That was the last rescue mission I'll do with you," whined Telgrin.

"Quit crying. You're alive, aren't you?" answered Sevran.

"I'm not crying."

Later on, Lonan and Kilgron stood in a hallway outside of the medical bay and watched Averine through the glass window while she slept.

"I'm very concerned about what you found. I don't know what's going on, but I think I know someone who does. We need to pay him a visit immediately," said Kilgron.

"Who?" asked Lonan.

"He goes by the name Armon, and he lives on planet 45x7."

"What? Are you serious? That planet is nothing but a ball of ice. How and why does he live there?" asked Lonan as they turned and walked down the hall.

"He wanted to stay out of sight. I knew him long ago, and I'm one of the only people who know of his location."

Just then Sevran and Telgrin walked out of the medical bay and into the hallway to meet up with them.

"How do you feel?" asked Lonan.

"Much better, but I need to get some fresh air," answered Sevran.

"Perfect, because you're coming with us to the luxurious planet 45x7," said Lonan with a smile.

"What? It's cold there," said Telgrin as they continued down the hallway.

"Quit crying. You're going," said Lonan.

"I'm not crying. I'm just saying it's really cold there. What's with everyone saying I'm crying?"

"Quit crying," said Sevran.

"I'm not crying!" shouted Telgrin as they rounded the corner back to the main hangar.

In one of the secondary hangar bays, the four men finished loading supplies into the Colt. Telgrin and Sevran had just finished tying down four small vehicles.

The vehicles were designed for transporting one soldier in snow-covered areas. They were shaped like the motorcycles but had three skis in the front instead of a tire. In the back was a pair of long metal tracks attached to the engine, which propelled it along the top of deep snow. SUSTs, which stood for Single-Unit Snow Transports, was the name Lonan had given them. Helion soldiers used them to patrol the enormous mountain ranges above their home.

Kilgron settled into the copilot's seat as Sevran and Telgrin strapped themselves into seats in the cargo bay. Lonan grabbed one last pack of weapons and headed toward the ship. Max had been watching them pack. He whined and stepped onto the ramp, wanting to accompany the team.

"No, Max, you stay here. It's too cold where we're going. Trust me, you would rather be here," Lonan said as he patted him on the head and continued up the cargo-bay ramp.

Seconds later the hover engines fired. They hovered out of the hangar into the morning sunlight and blasted off into the atmosphere. Planet 45x7 was within their star system, so the flight only took a few hours. Once they arrived, Lonan brought the Colt in for a landing in a small clearing halfway up the base of an enormous mountain range. The planet seemed to be covered in meters of snow. He found a clearing that was shielded by large trees that created a canopy. The winds blew with so much force that Lonan had a hard time hovering the Colt into a landing position.

Once he entered the cover of the trees, the winds died down, and he brought the ship in for a smooth touch down.

The younger men immediately went to work unloading the SUSTs while Kilgron gazed up into the mountain that loomed above them. The snow seemed to fall in waves and sheets as the powerful winds blew it in all directions.

"This is it."

"Are you sure?" asked Lonan as he finished strapping up his second-layer jacket. "How can anyone live here?"

"Yes, this is it. I recognize the description of the mountain peaks. He's here. We have a long way to go, so we need to get started."

They each mounted one of the SUSTs and followed Kilgron from the protection of the trees and up the steep mountain range. For many hours, they rode on through the rough terrain at a great speed. The higher they got, the greater the amount of snow that fell and the faster and harder the winds that blew. At some points, they put the SUSTs to the test as they climbed extremely steep cliffs.

Finally, after the sun had already set and night was only moments, away they arrived at a small, secluded cove created by two arms of the mountain. Nestled deep in back was a home built of stone and wood. It was nearly impossible to see, as it was covered in meters of snow. The mountain range around it was full of thick pine trees, which shielded it from the winds that now blew at such a constant speed that they had to yell to speak with one another. As they dismounted the SUSTs and walked toward the building, Kilgron yelled above the winds. "This may all be very new to you! I need you to be patient and listen carefully! I think that he is one of the only men who can help us!"

They all nodded as they tried to shield the snow from hitting them in the face.

As they drew closer to the building, they could see that the few small windows were lit with burning candles. The entrance was covered with a large vaulted roof that seemed to reach up into the mounds of snow that blanketed it. A black metal chandelier hung from the ceiling and was illuminated by twenty or thirty candles. Even though the wind blew so intensely, the light hung with little movement, as the entrance was well shielded.

The large, three-meter-tall dark-oak front door had black metal scrollwork on it. As they stepped into the protection of the roof of the entrance, the door opened before they had knocked or announced themselves.

Beautiful young Cloin stood before them. She greeted them with a very serious face.

"Welcome. Please come in. Armon thought you might be coming soon."

She stepped aside and opened the door wider as they entered. Kilgron entered first, and then Lonan, who was followed by Sevran, who smiled as he extended his hand and introduced himself.

"Hi, I'm Sevran, lead officer of the Helion Field Medical Units."

He expected his charm and smile to have their normal effect. However, Cloin ignored his hand and closed the door behind Telgrin as he shuffled in last.

He smiled as he whispered to Sevran, "See? I told you it was cold here."

"Shut up," grunted Sevran.

Telgrin smiled. He thoroughly enjoyed the fact that it was Sevran who was ignored by a woman for once.

As the foursome entered, they found the place to be warm and well lit with candles on the walls and more metal chandeliers hanging from the ceiling. The entrance was a long, wide hallway that was built with rough wood pillars that held up large timber rafters. The floor was made of dark slate tiles. The place was not refined in any way, but it was comfortable and inviting.

Cloin led them down the hallway and through a pair of large oak doors. The room that they entered appeared to be a library. The walls were lined with wooden shelves that extended to the ceiling and were filled with ancient-looking, leather-bound books. At the end of the room was a tall stone fireplace with a very healthy-looking fire. In front of it sat a wide wooden desk with three small piles of books on it.

At the desk sat an older man who looked like he might have been in his sixties. He was reading, but when they entered, he put down the book and greeted each of them with a warm handshake.

"Welcome, please come in."

He was a man of medium build, neither short nor tall. Even though the years seemed to be catching up with him, he didn't seem weak in any way. He shook their hands with the force of a twenty-year-old. And one could tell by the shape of his body that he had not been a weak man in his younger years. The scars on his hands, face, and neck also revealed that he had been a warrior.

"Armon, it's good to see you."

"Yes, it's been a long time," said Armon as he looked around at each of them.

"We have come because we need your help," said Kilgron.

"Yes, I know, please come," he said as he led them out of the room and down the hall. "Let's get you something warm to eat and drink. It's a little bit cold out there this time of year, isn't it?"

As they followed him out of the room, Sevran smiled again at Cloin. She just rolled her eyes as she turned and followed Armon. They walked to the other end of the hallway and through another pair of large oak doors.

They entered a wide dining room that had a long table and many chairs. An immense stone fireplace covered one wall at the end of the room and was surrounded by many soft, comfortable chairs. Armon led them to this end of the room and invited the men to sit and rest.

Just then Ahren, Cloin's brother, entered the room. He introduced himself and stood beside the fire with his sister.

Armon leaned against the fireplace and gazed into the flame as Kilgron told him everything that they had learned of the intruding army and what had happened in their latest rescue missions.

Moments into the story, a young man and woman entered the room. They brought food for each of the guests. The Helienders enjoyed hot venison and vegetable stew as they nearly melted into the comfort of the plush chairs and warm fire after a full day riding the SUSTs in the blistering cold.

Telgrin and Sevran worked hard to not fall asleep as Kilgron told Armon everything. Lonan nudged his younger brother to wake him up as Kilgron came to the end of the story.

"So that's the situation. There is an army of superhuman men that no one appears to be able to stop. I hoped that you could shed some light on this."

"Yes, I'll shed some light. Unfortunately I am fully aware of the problem. It's been growing for years, and I think it's reaching dangerous levels. It's like a cancer that spreads and grows out of control," said Armon as he reflectively gazed into the fire.

"What is it?" asked Lonan.

Armon turned to him and said, "We call it 'fear feeding.'"

Chapter 12

"What is that?" asked Kilgron.

"Let me describe it for you this way," continued Armon. "Have you ever noticed how an animal can sense that someone is evil? Or have you ever seen an infant cry simply because it can feel its mother's fear? This happens because our spirits emit this energy. The problem is that the enemy has found a way to absorb and harness that fear. And not only fear but despair, bitterness, hatred, greed, and all of mankind's evil. It gives him power. And the more evil mankind grows, the more powerful he becomes"

Cloin added, "The real problem, however, is that he has decided to take that power and invest it into the most evil men he can find. That's what's giving these soldiers the unnatural power that you've seen."

"Some of our older scholars believe that these men are Leviathan. Is that possible?" asked Kilgron.

"Not only possible but absolutely true," answered Armon. "The enemy has continually created new armies of Leviathan. After we defeat one, another arises elsewhere. The army that you speak of is led by a man they call Devakin. He is a ruthless Leviathan commander who has grown his forces to dangerous numbers.

The enemy has taken hold of a man by the name of Maginon. He is the leader of what you know as Nemaron. To the larger, more developed galaxies, they present themselves as a legitimate intergalactic company that supplies rare minerals, elements, and fuel. In reality they are just pawns that the enemy will dispose of when they are of no more use to him.

"He has used Nemaron to create a monopoly of the most precious elements that all civilizations need to survive. This has given them leverage to take over smaller star systems. Now they have amassed such wealth and power that they are able to simply take planets by force. This has allowed the enemy to grow his Leviathan army to a size we have never seen."

"Wait, wait. The enemy? Whose enemy? Who and what are you talking about?" asked Lonan.

Armon's voice became very clear and his face serious as he turned to Lonan. "There is a world that exists that you know nothing about. You cannot see it with your eyes. It is a hidden spirit world. In this world, there are forces for good and evil. They have been locked in a war for millennia, in what we call, 'the hidden battle.'"

Ahren added, "There are those who fight on our side. They protect us the best that they can, but mankind's evil has grown so great that they cannot fight both the enemy's forces and the evil forces of men.

"Maybe I should start at the beginning," said Armon as he sat down. "Please listen carefully, because what I am about to tell you can be hard for some to understand."

Armon paused for a moment as Cloin and Ahren drew up chairs.

"Mankind has been tormented by the oldest and greatest of evils for thousands upon thousands of generations. This evil has lain in the shadows, working in secret. He has existed for so long that very few know the truth of his origin.

"At the beginning of all things, the one God created countless galaxies and then made mankind in his image to inhabit many of them. There was peace among all men, and they lived in harmony with God. Before He made man and woman, He created angels to manage the galaxies. They were different from man in that they were immortal and had been endowed with many of His supernatural powers and abilities.

"God had created mankind and angels with free will. He wanted them to love and follow Him of their own choice. There was great peace and harmony in Heaven, as well as on the thousands of planets that God had created for man.

"However, evil began to stir in the heart of one of God's chief angels. The one who is called Satan grew envious of God's complete power. One ability that God had not given the angels was the power to create. This was the very thing that Satan began to crave with ever-increasing intensity. That craving grew and turned to jealousy—jealousy of the fact that mankind and angels loved God freely. As Satan's heart turned dark and twisted, he wanted nothing more than to be worshiped as if he were God."

Sevran paid special attention as Cloin took over the story.

"When God created the angels, He gave some the responsibility to be chiefs and leaders over others to help maintain order. They were also given a greater degree of strength and wisdom to help govern those under their care and direction. He made nine of them leaders, to which He gave each an equal part of the multitude of angels."

Armon continued, "Unfortunately, Satan was very capable in leadership and also in deception. As the evil in him continued to grow, he spoke lies against God and tried to create jealousy in the hearts of the other angels. One by one, they began to fall to the poison that had infected his mind. He convinced the others that they should have greater power and that God had been selfish in not giving them His ultimate power. He lied and promised them that, if they helped him to overthrow Heaven, they could share God's limitless power.

"Satan took advantage of his position of leadership and led many of the angels astray. He used those that he had corrupted to begin to build an army. In secret caves, they began to make weapons and armor. With each one they built, the evil mounted in them until it could be seen physically in their bodies. Their blood turned black and started to radiate from the center of their eyes.

"Then Satan came against opposition. Once, in a forest clearing in Heaven, he was refused, for the first time, by a group of three angels as he tried to convince them to follow him. As the three turned to walk way, Satan became furious. He pulled a knife and stabbed one of the angels in the back and through his heart.

"God had created them immortal with the ability to heal themselves. However, a blade to the heart or severing an angel's head would kill them. And with that, Satan had committed the first murder in the history of God's creation. The other two angels who had refused him grabbed Satan and threw him off their friend, but it was too late; he was dead. They picked him up and flew to the palace.

"The moment that it had happened, God had felt it. He summand His faithful angels, and they assembled in the large clearing below the palace.

"Satan stood in the forest clearing, with the bloody knife in his hand. The black blood pulsated through his eyes and crawled under his skin, as if maggots burrowed under his flesh. He and his fallen angels cowered in fear as they heard a trumpet blast from the palace. They took to flight in the opposite direction, back to the caves where they had been building and stockpiling their weapons.

"Satan's rash decision to kill had fast-forwarded his plan to attack the throne of God. He and his angels returned to their cave to collect their weapons and prepare for war.

"Back at the palace, God stood on the balcony overlooking the valley below. It broke his heart as he told his faithful angels what had happened. They turned to each other in disbelief and confusion. Just then, the two who had denied Satan flew to the balcony and laid the angel at God's feet. He shed a tear as He bent down and closed the eyes of the now dead angel.

"Then He stood, raised both His hands, and stretched them out toward the assembly before him. Instantly they were all fitted with armor: helmets, chest plates, thigh guards, and boots appeared on their bodies. In their hands, shields, swords, and spears materialized. Their horses also received chest plates, helmets, and shields across the base of their wings.

"Off in the distance, dark storm clouds began to form above the valley where Satan and his angels were gathering. Deep down in the valley, Satan's angels poured out of their caves and into the opening, where they lined up in formations. They had dressed themselves in the crude black armor that they had forged. Each of them carried long, sharp blades and wide, thick shields. The sockets of their eyes had turned to a deep bluish gray. The whites of their eyes had turned completely black.

"Satan flew up into the sky as the dark clouds behind him began to rumble and spit bolts of lightning. As he turned to look over his army, he lifted his right hand and filled it with a ball of fire. He then threw it at his angels. They raised their swords as the ball of fire spilled into thousands of small flames and landed on each of their blades. This ignited them in a deep-red blaze. Satan released a deep battle cry, which his angels responded to with their own.

"Then they all took to flight—some on horses and some by their own wings. They flew up into the clouds and seemed to ride the lightning as they turned toward the palace. This marked the beginning of the end, and there was war in Heaven.

"As God stood on the balcony, He watched as Satan and his angels flew toward the palace. He was filled with great sadness and righteous anger. He had foreseen that this day would come. He could see the evil growing in Satan's heart. He knew the ripple effect that it would have on the rest of His creation.

"Even though He had foreseen it, it did not dull the pain of what He knew was to come. His heart was broken as He shed another tear. But in the midst of that moment of deepest sadness, He looked over his angels who had remained faithful to him. He looked on the two who had denied Satan, and He was filled with joy. He was proud that some of His creation had remained faithful.

"Just then Satan and his angels raised their swords and launched fire from them. The fire converged into one massive ball of flame. It grew as it flew toward the palace, until it finally struck it and rained down flames over the balcony where God and some of his chief angels stood. The angels raised their shields to protect themselves. God didn't need to. The flames never went near him but were deflected by what looked like an invisible shield. God did not flinch or move at all. He only gazed at Satan and his army as they approached. There was no fear on His face, only disappointment and sadness.

"Down in the valley below, some of Satan's angels on horses had landed and formed a full cavalry charge. God's faithful angels mounted on horses rode out to meet them. As they charged toward their now evil brothers, they pulled their swords. The swords glowed with an intense blue light from pulsating lightning bolts.

"Satan's angels fired more balls of fire from their swords. The fire hit the shields of God's angels and scattered into millions of burning embers. Some made it past the shields and hit the angels, engulfing them entirely in flames. They dropped to the ground in agony as they rolled and tried desperately to put out the fire.

"God's angels returned fire as they shot massive bolts of lightning from the points of their blades. The bolts flew through the air and knocked Satan's angels to the ground, scorching them. Their bodies convulsed while the electrical current coursed through them. This burned their skin and burned off many of the feathers of their wings.

"On the balcony stood six of God's chief angels. They were the only leaders who had remained faithful. Satan was the seventh, and he had turned the other two. Tekel was one of the wisest and strongest of those that remained faithful to God. He flew down to the valley to join his angels in battle. Another of God's faithful leaders was Balim. He took to the sky to join the air defense.

"The battle was chaos. In the air and on the ground, the angels were locked in sword battle. They moved at speeds that could only be seen by heavenly eyes. Lightning bolts and flames flew in all directions.

"Satan led a legion of his demons through the air, where they collided with thousands of God's faithful. The collision was like the crashing of tremendous waves. Balim saw Satan and flew to engage him. Satan saw him coming and unleashed a stream of flame that would have killed any angels who got in its path. Balim raised his shield and pushed through the very center of the blaze.

"Satan stopped for a moment, thinking that he had destroyed Balim, only to find that he had flown through and was directly at the end of his blade. Balim caught Satan by surprise and hit him in the face with his shield. The impact was so great that it knocked Satan's helmet from his head and sent him tumbling out of the sky.

"The battle raged on. Both God's and Satan's angels were dying—some with a strategically placed sword thrust under the chest plate and into the heart and some with severed heads. The angels were equally matched in strength, so each army seemed to be losing equal numbers of soldiers. However, God's army was twice the size.

"Satan had only been able to get one-third of God's angels to follow him—the ninth under his command and that of the two chief angels he had poisoned, Abadol and Abafrile, and all the angels under them. Gradually God's angels were able to surround and corral their enemies.

"Tekel fought his way through many of Satan's angels to finally find him. When he did, he was standing over a pile of angels he had just slain. He stood with his back toward Tekel and held an injured angel in a headlock. He then took his sword and thrust it into the angel's chest. Satan let the body fall as he turned to Tekel and said, 'I'm sorry. Was he one of yours?'

"They squared off and began to circle one another.

"'How can you be so foolish? What could you hope to accomplish?' asked Tekel.

"'Accomplish?' replied Satan. 'One day, you will all bow down and worship me!'

As he said this, Satan raised his shield and sword and took a battle stance. Tekel didn't respond but remained calm, with his arms at his sides. Behind him two of Satan's angels silently charged toward Tekel's back. At the same time, Satan charged from the opposite direction. Tekel raised his shield and took a defensive position to oppose Satan, still apparently not aware of the attack coming from behind.

"Then, just seconds before Satan's angels hit him from the back, Tekel spun around in a low position and blocked the first angel's strike with his shield while taking off both the attackers' legs with one smooth blow. Still in a low position, he then thrust his blade up under the chest plate of the second attacker.

"With his blade raised high, Satan still charged from the other direction. At the last second, just before he reached Tekel, Balim flew down and blocked Satan's sword thrust with his blade. He then punched Satan in the face so hard that he flew backward several meters. Tekel turned to defend himself against two more of Satan's angels. Satan jumped back to his feet as he and Balim engaged in sword combat. Their movements were so fast that their blades and hands were no more than a blur.

"Just then something happened. The entire battlefield simultaneously slowed in motion. God himself had appeared in the middle of the battle. He walked at a normal speed, but he had slowed time to the point that all motion had almost entirely stopped. As He walked, His face was filled with great sadness as He looked at the death and destruction. God stood beside Satan and Balim as they were nearly frozen in time.

"The two angels could see God standing beside them. Satan turned his attention toward God. Even though he could barely move, he tried to swing his sword in God's direction and attack Him.

"God raised his hand and said, 'Enough.'

"And with the slightest movement, He created a shock wave that sent Satan flying backward twenty meters. At that moment, everything went back to normal speed.

"A great wind began to blow. At the far side of the battlefield, behind Satan and his forces, a black hole appeared. The wind swirled around the hole and forced everything toward it. God's angels continued to surround and corral Satan's army as they drove them back toward what could now be recognized as a portal to the created world.

"'You are hereby banished,' said God as He stood unaffected by the wind while everyone around Him struggled to stay on their feet.

"Then all of Satan's angels were picked up by the wind and forced through the portal. Their horses were also pulled in. God's angels continued to drive them back until all were gone except for Satan, Abadol, and Abafrile. They tried to stand their ground against the incredible winds while all of God's angels stood and watched.

"Satan stood and stared back at all of them, with no remorse on his face, only hatred and envy as he yelled above the rush of the wind: "I will return to rule this place!"

"God raised His right hand and again made a slight gesture with His fingers, which finally sent Satan and his angels falling backward through the portal. As they passed through, the hole began to shrink, and the winds also slowed.

"As the portal closed completely, the winds stopped. The angels looked around in disbelief. The battle was over, but the war had only begun."

Chapter 13

Armon continued, "Inside the portal, Satan and his angels fell through a tunnel with sides that were made of what appeared to be great, powerful winds. They tried to fly, but the winds were too strong, and they tumbled like rag dolls. As they neared the end, they could see planets far off in the distance, and through the walls, they could nearly make out the shine of distant stars.

"As they exited the end of the tunnel, they found themselves falling through outer space in one of God's created galaxies. We now call it 55X13. They had been cast down to the created world. As they fell, they neared a small volcanic planet that was covered in lava and ash. When they entered its atmosphere, they each became engulfed in flames.

"Their bodies went through a transformation. Their wings were entirely burned off, and their bodies became warped and distorted. The blackish blue color that started at their eyes now covered their entire bodies. Their eyes turned to a bright-red flame.

"The horses also were changed. Their skin and feathers burned off, and fangs began to appear in their mouths.

"They all crashed into the surface of a volcanic planet. Satan, Abadol, and Mammelel landed together and created an enormous crater as they crashed through the upper crust and landed in a deep lake of lava in an underground cavern.

"Back in Heaven, Tekel and Balim spoke with the other chief angels. They agreed that they didn't want to take the chance of falling prey to Satan's abilities to tempt others to his evil path. So they surrendered their free will to God. They requested that He remove it so that they could better serve Him as they go to creation to protect their human brothers. God was impressed with their willingness to sacrifice.

"At that moment, all the angels bowed on one knee. God waved His hand above them and sent out a blazing white light across the entire multitude that had assembled before Him.

"As He did this, it erased all potential for evil and sin. They became united and are now always one with God and His spirit. He loves mankind and, therefore, so do they. God sent them here to protect us until the appointed time when Satan will be destroyed and with him all evil. Then all of God's creation will once again be at peace.

"When Satan fell, he took a third of God's angels with him. God sent half of His remaining angels to creation. They have been assigned to protect different solar systems and are spread across the galaxies. God's creation is enormous—far larger than we can fathom.

"Satan has built an army upon the evil and greed that he planted in the hearts of men. He plays with man's free will and lies to him until evil takes hold and begins to grow.

"That is what's happening now. He has amassed so much evil and suffering that his soldiers are twice as powerful as they once were. And the men that he has turned are many times more powerful than a normal human man."

Armon had completed his account and waited for his guests' responses. Sevran and Telgrin looked confused. Lonan, on the other hand, looked very skeptical.

Sevran asked, "So you're saying that those Leviathan soldiers that we have come up against are powered by fallen angels?"

Ahren answered, "Not really. You saw the machine with the red globe mounted in the ceiling of the slave compound where they held you captive?"

"Yeah, I saw it."

Cloin interjected: "That's what the enemy uses to absorb the fear and hate from mankind. It gives him strength. As he gets stronger, he then puts some of that power into evil men and uses them to do his will. These are what we call Leviathans."

Armon added, "These machines also absorb the pain and suffering that we experience in death. That is why he hangs the captives the way that he does. He does simultaneous executions and absorbs massive amounts of suffering at that time. This gives him what we call a 'death boost,' which is an additional dose of evil power."

Ahren said, "We've seen him use this at times when he's preparing for a large-scale attack. It's usually shrouded by human war and genocide. But he's becoming more organized and calculating in his attacks."

Armon said, "This brings me to something very important that I must tell you. There is something that you and your rescue teams have been doing wrong. You must not kill the enemy's soldiers. It only adds to his power. We use very powerful tranquilizing darts. They work, but not very well against large armies."

"We've seen that you're very talented in creating and engineering new weapons," said Ahren. "But you need to create those that don't kill."

Telgrin spoke up and asked, "I saw red-globe machines at the slave camp on Tarnus. Why would he use them there?"

Armon answered, "The camps are filled with misery, despair, fear, and death. These poor souls are living out a miserable existence. He collects tremendous amounts of power in these places."

Cloin added, "While also giving slave labor to his evil human pawns so that they can enlarge their systems of control and dominance throughout the galaxies."

"Why don't you just destroy the machines?" asked Sevran.

"We've tried that and failed. As they are being used, they are too full of power and cannot be destroyed. If the source of fear and misery is removed, then they are vulnerable to attack," answered Cloin.

"Wait," Lonan interjected. "How did you know they were taken captive in one of the slave compounds? We didn't tell you that."

"We were there helping you," said Ahren. "We've been with you many times on your missions."

"We are Seberians," said Cloin. "A group of men and women that God has trained and gifted to fight the evil forces of not only mankind but also Satan."

"The hand of God is moving in this galaxy," said Armon. "Our planet and our force have been named Seber, and with reason. The word means 'hope' in some ancient tongues of men, and it is through this hope that he will free mankind from the oppression of Satan."

"Our small army works from in the shadows," said Ahren. "And we're not the only ones there helping you."

"Wait, wait," interrupted Lonan. "I think I know what you're going to say. I have a hard time believing any of this. Are you trying to tell me that God sends supernatural beings here to help us? If that's the case, why do I see nothing but death and destruction all around the galaxies? Why do I see nothing but pain and suffering?" Lonan stood as he became more aggravated. "And why were our parents murdered when we were just kids?"

"Hey, man, relax," said Sevran as he grabbed Lonan's arm.

"No, I won't relax!" yelled Lonan as he pulled his arm away. "I don't want to sit here and listen to these nut jobs. I don't believe you, and I think you're all crazy!" he shouted as he paced around the room in frustration.

"Would you like to see?" asked Armon.

"See? See what?" demanded Lonan. He turned to Sevran and said, "Look, he's crazy!"

Just then Tekel and two other huge angels stepped through a portal and into the room. The awesome sight of them so frightened the men that Sevran and Telgrin fell backward as they flipped over their chairs. Kilgron jumped to his feet and stepped back several meters. Lonan was so startled that he pulled his handgun and fired six shots at Tekel, who caught the bullets in his hand.

In a flash, the second angel, Balim, appeared by Lonan's side and grabbed the gun. He crushed it with one hand as Tekel allowed the bullets to fall to the floor.

"All of you need to relax. Humans never can get over the sight of us," said Genon. His voice was deep and echoed in their ears.

Genon was the third angel that had appeared. He was not a chief of the angels. He had been a subordinate to Satan and was the one and only of them who had not succumbed to his poison. He had also been among the three that denied Satan in the forest of Heaven and had witnessed the first murder. He knew Satan better than anyone and was now a great help to Tekel as he led God's forces.

"Well, *you're* ugly," replied Balim, whose voice was more massive than Genon's. When he and Tekel spoke, it sounded as though ten men were speaking.

"Thanks," answered Genon with a grin.

The four men stood and stared in disbelief and said nothing for a long while. Armon, Cloin, and Ahren showed no alarm because they knew the angels well.

After a time of silence, Lonan spoke up and said, "They must have put something in our drinks. They've drugged us."

"I didn't drink anything, and I'm seeing what you're seeing," said Sevran.

"Well, then they put it in our food," returned Lonan.

"Peace," said Tekel as he raised his right hand in an attempt to calm them. "We mean you no harm." His voice boomed and echoed throughout the room. "Maybe we should change our appearance to something you are more accustomed to."

As he said this, his voice seemed to dissolve down to the human voice of one man. The intense white light of their eyes dimmed until they revealed crystal-blue human eyes underneath.

Armon stepped forward and said, "These are some of God's highest-ranking angels. Gentleman, meet Tekel, Balim, and Genon."

There was a long silence until Telgrin asked, "So the fallen angels you talked about, do they don't look like these guys?"

"They once did but no more," answered Ahren.

"Come with us," said Tekel as he grabbed Lonan and Sevran by the arms and nearly carried them outside.

Moments later they all stood on the wide flat ledge in front of the building. It was very early morning. They had been talking all night, and the sun had not yet come up over the horizon. From this very high point, they could see for hundreds of kilometers off into the distance. The wind had subsided during the night, and only a faint bit of snow gently blew across their faces as they looked out across the vast valley.

"Look up into the morning sky," said Tekel. "There is your home planet of Helion. Do you see it?"

"Yes," they all answered.

"Look very closely." As Tekel said this, he passed his hand across Lonan's face. The other two angels did the same for the other men. At that moment, it seemed as if something had fallen from their eyes. Their vision changed. They seemed to pass through space and arrive on their home planet. They could see the top of the mountain that was their home. Above it they could also see fifteen demons flying around, circling in the air above their home. They flew on massive bat-like wings. The men could now see with eyes like eagles. Even though they were on a completely different planet, it was as if their eyes could zoom in to the point that they were only two or three meters away.

The sight of the demons was so horrific that it seemed to tear the breath from their lungs. They could see, with great clarity, every detail that had been described to them in the story of the demons' fall from Heaven. They were massive warriors. Their flesh was charred, their eyes emitted an intense red light, and their blades burned with a deep-orange and red flame.

Then in a flash, fifteen angels flew from the mountain below and met the demons above in midair combat. Their blades clashed in a spectacle of light and flame. Moments later the demons abandoned their attack and were driven off by the angels.

"Demons are there?" asked Telgrin in amazement.

"We fight them off continually. But recently they found your home and their attacks have become more frequent," said Balim.

"This is what goes on that you don't see," said Ahren.

Just then Lonan's mind took him back to a moment on Tarnus when the Leviathan soldier mysteriously disappeared before his eyes as a shadow flew across his path. He snapped from this vision and back to reality as he heard Tekel's deep voice: "You see now, don't you?"

Chapter 14

A great distance away on Satan's volcanic planet, things began to stir. Deep down under the surface, he sat on his throne as tremendous noise grew outside of the tunnel entrance. There was a roar of thousands of wings that steadily grew until thousands of demons landed outside the throne room. One of Satan's attendants approached the throne to report. "My lord, the reinforcements from the neighboring galaxies have arrived."

Two very large warrior demons led the pack as they entered. Their names were Abaddon and Abadile. Once they had been two of God's chief angels—equals with Satan. But now that they had been cast down to creation, they had become captains of his armies. They had each been assigned particular galaxies in which to oppress and torment mankind. Very often there were arguments over territorial lines. Abaddon stepped forward.

"You summoned us?" He tried to hide his distain. He didn't like taking orders—none of the demons did. They all thought that they could rule better than Satan. There was a great deal of infighting in their ranks, but Satan was able to maintain power and keep them all in check.

Satan stood and stepped forward from the shadow, revealing his horrific face. His eyes surged with red-hot intensity as he said, "Yes. Our time has come."

He was completely covered in crude, heavy armor. His wings remained furrowed behind him but were still so large that they reached several meters above his head. He was larger than any of the other demons.

"It is time for us to enter through the great gate and claim the throne of Heaven."

Abaddon and Abadile both grinned, and the rest of the demons roared in delight.

Back on planet Seber, everyone had returned to the dining area of Armon's mountain home. The men warmed themselves by the fire as Tekel spoke.

"It has always been Satan's goal to return to Heaven and try to take the throne from God. We believe that he has found the hidden location of the gateway."

Balim added, "With the amount of power he has collected, we think that he will try to fight his way through us and into the gate."

"We need your help to stop his men," said Genon. "We don't want to destroy them. Satan uses his human soldiers as pawns. He sends them to fight us just to get in our way. That's what prevents us from protecting the rest of mankind."

Tekel added, "We can kill these men, but God does not want us to. They are blinded by the enemy and must be set free from his bondage."

"Satan has built his army, and now mankind is forced to take action," said Armon.

Cloin interjected, "Maginon and his Leviathan army have their eye on your planet. You are next in line to be taken over. Your home is rich in natural resources, and they know that. It's only a matter of time until your people are taken as slaves and your beautiful planet destroyed."

"What do you need us to do?" asked Lonan.

"We need to coordinate rescue missions that will free the slaves and remove Satan's extra power," said Armon. "When we do that, the Leviathan will lose their power, and we'll have an even fight."

"We'll still be outnumbered," added Telgrin.

"Yeah, but I would rather fight them as regular men," said Sevran.

"But you need to use weapons that don't add to his power. We must not kill his soldiers," said Ahren.

"Well, not a lot of them anyway," said Cloin with a grin.

"We will meet Satan and his forces at the gate," said Tekel. "That will keep his attention as you sneak in and shut down the camps. Free the slaves, and you will protect your people."

Kilgron turned to the others and said, "We have no time to waste. We have a great deal of work to do: shuttles and fighters to convert to hydrocell—"

"Missions to plan," interrupted Sevran

"Weapons to design and build," said Lonan.

"Yeah, we should get going," said Telgrin. "Back to Helion, where it's warm." He shuttered and rubbed his arms to warm himself as they filed out of the room.

Just then Lonan looked across the room and saw an angel's chest plate and armor leaning against the wall. He turned to Tekel and asked, "Can I barrow that?" He pointed to the armor.

"You can have it."

"Thanks," said Lonan.

He tried to pick up the chest plate, but it was extremely heavy.

"Hey, come help me with this," he said to his brother. Sevran and Telgrin came and helped him carry it out of the room.

In another galaxy, the Nemaron command ship orbited a small planet that it had just finished attacking. Flames and smoke poured from the major cities as Nemaron transport shuttles carried away captives.

Inside Maginon's chamber, he and his highest-ranking officers sat around a large table in his conference room. Devakin was there with many of his military officers. The men were speaking among themselves when suddenly the lights dimmed and flickered. They went out for a moment, and the room was completely black. They came back on, and everyone looked around confused. Suddenly they went out again, and when they came back on, Satan and five of his demons were standing on the table. One of the demons had his face directly in front of Maginon's assistant's face. The assistant was so scared that he fell backward in his chair. The demons laughed as they flew down off the table and began to circle the men. Satan landed at the far end of the room and turned to face Maginon.

"The time has come for our attack on the great gate," said Satan. "You will attack Helion at the same time. That will force those servants of Him to divide their army as they try to protect their precious little friends."

"Yes, my lord. We've already planned the attack, and we are positioning our assets as we speak," answered Maginon with slight crack in his voice. As he spoke, one of the demons was moving very near to him, almost as if smelling him.

Satan strolled to the side of the conference room and looked out the window as he said, "Good. I'm not surprised that you are already prepared. I've seen your mouth watering for their resources."

Satan gazed out the window and enjoyed watching the Nemaron soldiers finishing their attack on the now helpless planet below. They could still see explosions and smoke billowing from the surface as their attack ships moved back and forth, carrying captives and soldiers.

"Yes, my lord," Maginon nervously responded.

"I don't need to remind you of the consequences of failure," said Satan as his eyes burned a deeper red.

"No, my lord,"

"Good. Then we shall leave you to continue your work."

Satan unfurled his powerful wings and took to the air, hovering just three feet above the ground. The demon that had been hovering so closely to Maginon turned and looked at Satan in disappointment.

"You said we could have at least one."

The men looked up in horror.

"One," said Satan.

Instantly the demon grabbed a man sitting directly next to Maginon by the head and flew up through the ceiling. The man screamed as one of his shoes fell and landed on the table while the rest of him disappeared through the ceiling. The other men stared at the shoe in disbelief while the rest of the demons followed up through the ceiling.

"Don't fail me," said Satan as he beat his powerful wings and also flew up through the ceiling.

Back at Helion, Averine was in the medical bay finishing getting dressed when Lonan walked in.

"How you feeling?" asked Lonan as he kissed her.

"Great. I'm ready to get back to work. Where have you been?"

"Come on, I've got a lot to fill you in on. You got some rest, right?"

"Yeah," she answered with an inquisitive look.

"Good, you're going to need it. We have a lot of work to do," said Lonan as they walked out of the medical bay and down the hall.

Later that day in the main hangar, Telgrin, Sevran, Lonan, and hundreds of other mechanics and engineers worked feverishly to convert shuttles, fighters, AUVs, Stingers, and motorcycles to hydrocell engines. Lonan rolled out from underneath a Stinger with tools in his hand. He put them away and then turned to a computer monitor to check some readings.

Just then something grabbed his attention. Leaning against the wall was the angelic armor that he had been given on planet Seber.

"Hey, grab that rifle for me," Lonan said to Sevran.

He picked up a rifle that was standing in a weapons case and handed it to his brother.

"Sure. What are you doing?"

Lonan took aim at the chest plate in the corner and fired a burst of rounds. The shot was loud, and everyone in the hangar stopped working and looked to see what was going on.

"Is he crazy?" they heard one of the men murmur.

"Everything's all right. I'm just running a little test," Lonan said.

"Shouldn't you being doing that down in the range?" asked Telgrin.

"It's OK. I've got a hunch," answered Lonan.

The three of them walked to the chest plate to examine it and found it in perfect condition.

"Those rounds didn't do a thing. No holes, no dents, nothing, and look." Lonan reached down and picked up three rounds. "They don't ricochet. It seems to absorb the impact," said Lonan.

"No chance of something bouncing up and hitting them in the face. Like a sword," said Telgrin.

"Take this outside. I want to try something else," ordered Lonan.

As they struggled to carry the chest plate outside, Lonan rolled up in one of the AUVs. He parked it and took aim with one of the large, fully automatic guns while the other two draped the chest plate over a rock so that it would stand upright.

"You might want to get out of the way," said Lonan, sending the other two running for cover.

Lonan fired a dozen large-caliber rounds into the chest plate. When the dust cleared, Sevran and Telgrin walked over and examined it. By now a group of engineers and mechanics had gathered by the door to watch.

"You're going to have to try harder. You got nothing!" said Sevran.

"Try the cannons," yelled Telgrin.

Lonan climbed up into the gun turret as the others ran for cover again. From within the turret, Lonan locked the chest plate into the targeting system and fired. The missile flew through the air and hit its target dead center.

When the dust cleared, they could see that the rock had been pulverized, and the chest plate was covered in rubble. Lonan got out of the AUV while Telgrin and Sevran came out from hiding. They all walked over to inspect the damage. Lonan wiped the dust and debris from it and found nothing.

"I can't believe it. No damage. OK, one more test," said Lonan.

Back inside the shop of the main hangar, they struggled to lift the chest plate into a large secure box with clear panels on all sides. Lonan pushed some keys at the control panel, and a laser torch moved into position and pointed directly at the chest plate.

The laser then ignited and fired a constant beam at the very center of the chest plate for several seconds. Lonan turned it off and opened the panel to examine it. The three men stared in amazement, finding no damage at all. Not even charring.

"You've got to be kidding me!" said Sevran.

"OK, enough messing around. Let's get back to work," said Lonan. As the others went back to work, Lonan stood and stared with the most puzzled look on his face.

Much later that night, Lonan was up very late working in the lab. As he sat working at a computer station, he fought hard to stay awake until he finally set his head down for just a second and quickly drifted off.

As he slept, he slipped into a strange dream. He found himself standing on a sandy hill that overlooked ruins of a vast city. Red and orange clouds rolled across the sky at an unusually fast speed.

Then he heard a voice: "Free the captives, and release those who are trapped in darkness."

He turned to see who had said it but found no one.

Just then he jumped from his sleep and found himself still sitting at the workstation in the lab. It was morning, and the sun was just coming up. Telgrin walked in carrying food and drinks.

"Wow. Have you been here all night?"

"Unfortunately," answered Lonan as he rubbed his bloodshot eyes.

"And you slept like that? Your neck is going to feel great. Here, have some coffee."

"Thanks," said Lonan.

Later that day, Lonan walked into the main counsel chamber, where his wife, Kilgron, Armon, Ahren, and Cloin stood around the table. They were reviewing details of the slave camps and planning the rescue missions.

"How's it going?" asked Lonan.

"OK, how about you?" asked Averine.

"I'm working on a weapon plan, but I need some help." He turned to Armon and asked, "Do you have any more angel armor?"

"I don't, but I know where we could find it. Why?"

"I have an idea, and I want to look into it now. Can you tell me how to find it?"

Armon looked at him inquisitively and answered, "No. But I'll take you there."

"OK, let's go."

Hours later the men had loaded into a small shuttle and were entering the outer limits of a neighboring galaxy. Lonan piloted while Armon sat in the copilot seat, navigating and showing him the way. Ahren was sitting behind them, in the back of the cockpit.

Between the two pilots' seats, the holographic navigation system projected images of the entire star system that they were entering. The computer scanned the planets and moons and began to give technical data on each.

Armon pointed at one moon that was orbiting a large plant near the center of the system. The computer highlighted that moon and then zoomed in closer.

"That's the one, the third moon of this planet. It's called Malton. Land in the fourth quadrant of the southwestern hemisphere. There," said Armon as he zoomed into the specific area on the moon.

Lonan brought the shuttle in for a smooth landing in what looked like a desert. Ruins of an abandoned city lay in the background. The cargo bay of the shuttle opened, and the three men filed out. With just a quick glance, one could tell that a great global war had taken place there long ago. The buildings had not only decayed but had blast markings and holes that had obviously been made by massive weapons.

"It's over here," said Armon as he led the men up and over a large sand dune.

As they came to the top, they looked down to find the valley filled with angel and demon armor that almost entirely covered the ground. Alongside the armor were human skeletal remains. It was obvious that a very bloody battle had taken place there. Lonan had a strange feeling as he turned and looked back over the ruins behind them.

"I think I've seen this place before." He paused and looked around. "In a dream." He struggled to understand how.

"Really? When?" asked Armon.

"Just last night," said Lonan as he became even more confused.

Ahren and Armon shared a quick glance.

"This was the scene of a terrible battle. As you can see, many angels died. As did many humans," said Armon as he looked across the valley.

"What happened here?" asked Lonan.

"A long time ago, Satan lured many planetary leaders and scientists to this place," explained Armon. "He had poisoned the mind of the leader of this planet, and he used him to bring these people for a humanitarian meeting concerning energy and power supplies. Satan and hundreds of his demons had built a perimeter around the city.

"Balim was caretaker of this star system. He and hundreds of his angels, along with a small army of the first of the Seberian soldiers, tried to fight their way through the ranks of Satan to save the men and women in the city. This is where that battle took place. But while there was so much death and destruction in the city behind them, Satan and his demons absorbed such levels of evil that Balim and his angels couldn't make it through to save the humans."

"Why would they bring leaders from other star systems?" asked Lonan.

"These leaders and scientists were some of the brightest minds in the neighboring galaxies, and their discoveries threatened the monopoly that this planet was enjoying," said Armon.

"Wait," said Lonan as a look of dread and alarm came over his face. "If they were scientists, were my parents…" He paused.

"Yes, your parents were both killed in that city behind you," said Armon as he pointed in the direction of the ruins.

As he did, Lonan spun around and sat down on the top of the sand dune. He gazed at the ruins as he tried to process what he had just heard.

"All the leaders and scientists who had been lured here were murdered by Satan's human soldiers deep inside the walls of the city. I'm sorry that you learned of it in this way."

"All they would ever tell me was that they died on a mission."

After several minutes of silence, Lonan asked, "Where are the men who did it? Where are the men who killed my parents?"

"They are all gone," answered Ahren. "Within two years, this planet was engulfed in total planetary war. All the men involved in their murder are dead. There is no one on whom you can take revenge—if that is what you are thinking. Besides, that's not a road you want to walk down. It would only leave you emptier than when you began."

"I didn't ask you!" snapped Lonan as he jumped to his feet.

"Ahren's parents died here as well," said Armon. "I was here fighting alongside Balim and his angels as a soldier of Seber. We tried to save your family and this planet, but the enemy and his forces were too great. Over there on that ridge, I was locked in a deadly battle with a particularly powerful demon."

Armon pointed off to the far side of the battlefield.

"He had beat me to the ground and was about to kill me. The demon raised his blade high and prepared to thrust it into my heart, when suddenly Balim came to my aid and cut off the demon's sword-wielding hand. He then quickly ended the demon's miserable existence by severing his head.

"'Retreat, the battle is lost.' Balim shouted to me as he lifted me to my feet. 'All the humans are dead. There is nothing left to fight for!'

"He and the angels provided cover as the few remaining men retreated. As I ran back toward my ship, I passed a small house and heard two children crying. That's where I found Ahren and Cloin. Ahren was four years old and was holding his one-month-old sister. Their parents had been killed. Their mother had shielded them with her body and saved their lives. I rescued them, took them home, and raised them as my own children."

Lonan turned and looked at Ahren with newfound compassion. "Sorry."

Ahren just nodded in acceptance.

Lonan lowered his head and thought deeply as he tried to process all that he had just learned.

"This Satan you speak of…he was involved? He was the mastermind?"

"Yes, but you can't have revenge on him. God will do that one day. You need to focus on protecting your people," answered Armon.

"You're right," said Lonan as he pulled a floating stretcher from his pack, opened it, and started loading angel and demon armor. "That's why I don't like to get involved with other planets. We should just stay home and take care of ourselves. Let's get what we came for and get out of here."

Armon watched with deep sadness as Lonan and Ahren began to load the armor.

Chapter 15

Back at the mountain sanctuary on planet Seber, Tekel stood on the ledge that overlooked the valley below as Balim approached him from behind.

"You called?" asked Balim.

"Yes. I need you to take special care of Lonan. He doesn't know it, but his people need his help."

Balim lowered his eyes.

"Yes, sir. I will do my best." He still felt a hint of shame over the loss of the many humans at the battle on planet Malton.

"I believe you are the best warrior for the job," said Tekel.

"Thank you, sir."

Lonan had finished loading a large quantity of angelic armor with the help of Ahren and Armon. Once they finished, they took the long trip back to their solar system, with Lonan piloting the shuttle toward the space between the two suns. Suddenly the shuttle's computer system sounded an alarm.

"What's that?" asked Ahren.

"We're entering a dangerous area," answered Lonan. "This is the time in our planetary cycle when our suns are the most near to one another. The area in between is full of solar flares and intense heat, which means that it's time to stop and let the machines do the rest."

He stopped the shuttle and turned on autopilot, which maintained their orbit outside of the danger zone. He then went to the back of the cockpit and sat down at another control station and started loading some commands.

"What are you doing?" asked Ahren.

"Just watch, and you'll see."

On the bottom side of the ship, a hatch opened. From it flew a spherical satellite that continued on toward the area between the suns. As it traveled, a yellow force field appeared around its outer layer. Its color intensified until it was a deep orange.

"OK, little buddy, hold together," said Lonan as he watched on the monitor inside the cockpit.

The satellite finally came to a stop when its outer shield burned red hot. It then began to transform its shape. It split around its circumference, and the two halves separated. As it did, it revealed a pile of armor lying on a platform inside. The now open section did not have a shield covering it, so the armor was directly exposed to the solar radiation. Seconds later the shield burned with such intensity that it began to break down and dissolve. Immediately another shield was emitted from within the sphere, the second one was a bright blue.

"One down, three to go," said Lonan as he punched some keys at the control station.

After several minutes, the armor on the inside started to glow bright orange, and the thinner outer parts of the armor started to melt. As they did, the liquid, heavenly metal was drawn down through a tube that led to a small storage chamber in the bottom of the satellite. In that chamber, the liquid flowed down into channels.

From his screen inside, Lonan could see all this happening as the computer monitored the process.

"Yes, it's working."

"What's working? What are you doing?" asked Armon.

"Don't worry. You'll see in just a minute. We'd better get the other satellites ready. Come with me; I could use your help," said Lonan as the men followed him out of the cockpit and into the cargo bay.

On the Nemaron command ship, Devakin stood on a control balcony that looked out over a vast hangar located on the port side of the ship. This command ship also doubled as a carrier, so the hangar was filled with hundreds of Nemaron fighters and soldier transports. The far end of the hangar was open to space, and more transports were entering through it. Devakin was speaking with one of his subordinates when Maginon entered with two armed guards.

"Have you assembled all the men?" asked Maginon.

"Yes, sir. Everything is on schedule. We're gathering our soldiers from all over the galaxy."

"Good," said Maginon as he stepped to the edge of the balcony and looked down to see hundreds of thousands of men standing in formations. Hundreds more poured into the hangar as they marched from the inner parts of the ship while the rest loaded onto the soldier transports.

Back on planet Helion, Lonan dumped a container of bullets onto a table in the shooting range buried deep under the mountain. Sevran, Averine, Telgrin, Kilgron, Cloin, Armon, and Ahren were all there to watch his demonstration.

"OK, these are the rounds I made from melting down the heavenly metal used to make the angel armor," said Lonan as he loaded the bullets one at a time into his rifle.

"You really think this is going to work? We shot that thing with an AUV cannon," said Sevran.

"Yeah, I think it's going to work. Can you set it up for me?"

Telgrin and Sevran lifted the angel chest plate onto a motorized trailer and stood it upright. Then using a remote control, Telgrin drove the trailer down to the other end of the shooting range, where it rested against the wall.

"Clear," said Lonan as he took aim.

Everyone took a few steps back and covered their ears as Lonan fired his rifle. As the round exited the barrel, it kicked Lonan back much more than normal. As it flew through the air, it left a thin silver mist behind it. Lonan reeled in pain as he tried to collect himself from the unexpected kick.

"Ha-ha, did you feel that? Looked like it hurt," said Sevran, laughing.

"Wow. I've never felt recoil like that before."

"You've never worked with metal like this before," added Armon.

"Telgrin, bring it back. I'm going to need to reengineer the rifle to absorb some of that," said Lonan as he rubbed his shoulder.

The trailer came back to them, and they examined the chest plate. They found three bullet holes in the center of it.

"That's what I wanted to see. Now, if there are any demons at the slave camps, we'll have something to fight back with," said Lonan.

"But you won't be able to see them," said Ahren.

"Only my Seberians, with their training and abilities, will be able to see and hit demons," added Armon.

"I know. I made these rounds for your men," Lonan said. He looked at Cloin and corrected himself: "I mean your soldiers. But our people can use them also…look." He pointed down to the computer screen and showed them the technical data on the shots he had just fired.

"Those rounds are twice as fast as our regular ones," said Telgrin as he examined the data.

"But you need something that doesn't kill," said Cloin.

"One of the problems is the fact that the Leviathan soldiers are so fast that they can dodge our rounds. If we mount this new immobilizing head on these heavenly metal rounds, our guys can hit them. Or at least come closer," explained Lonan.

"What immobilizing heads?" asked Sevran.

"I'm glad you asked. Go stand down range, and I'll show you."

"No thanks."

Lonan pulled a round from another clip and showed the group. "These carry enough electrical current to knock out a full-grown man for five to six hours. It won't kill them, just knock them out cold," said Lonan as he glanced at Cloin. "Let me show you. I knew I wouldn't be able to get a volunteer, so I brought someone else."

He reached down and pushed some keys at the computer station. At the far end of the range, a small hatch opened. Lonan raised his rifle and took aim. For several seconds, nothing happened.

Suddenly they could see the metallic silver reflection of two eyes peering from the darkness. An instant later, a two-meter-tall wolf charged out of the hatch and ran toward the group at full attack speed. Nothing stood between them and the wolf except the empty floor of the shooting range. Lonan found the wolf in his scope while everyone else jumped backward and started to panic.

Ahren raised his rifle to fire when Lonan shouted, "Wait, don't shoot!"

Lonan fired a shot, but the wolf continued its charge. He had missed. "Oops," said Lonan as he took more careful aim.

From behind him, Sevran yelled, "What are you doing, man? Shoot it!"

Lonan fired another round and, this time, hit the wolf in the neck. An electrical current surged through the animal's body. Instantly it fell asleep. It fell to the floor, sliding from its momentum, until it finally came to a stop just centimeters from Lonan's feet.

He turned to the worried group behind him and said, "I could have hit it the first time. I was just playing with you." As he turned back to the wolf, his raised eyebrows proved otherwise.

"Not funny," said Telgrin as the others stepped forward cautiously. He stooped down and examined the wolf more closely. "Won't the power of those rounds cause it to go right through the skin?"

"No. I designed them with a specially engineered blunt tip so that they won't kill anyone. But they'll definitely hurt," answered Lonan.

Telgrin reached over to touch the wolf when Lonan yelled, "No, wait don't!"

The moment Telgrin touched the hair of the wolf, he received a serious electric shock. The current threw him backward a meter but wasn't enough to knock him out.

"Wow!" yelled Telgrin.

Sevran and Averine tried not to laugh.

"I tried to tell you. Don't touch."

"Is the wolf OK?" asked Averine as she reached over to try to get a closer look.

"He's fine. He's just sleeping. We'll release him back into the wild later," answered Lonan.

"OK, enough of this hands-on presentation. What is our battle-ready status?" asked Kilgron.

Sevran answered, "All shuttle, fighter, and vehicle conversions are well under way. We should be done by the end of the day tomorrow."

"We're nearly done with our missile interceptors," said Telgrin as he tried to shake the pain from his hand.

"We need to take a team to retrieve more armor so that I can make more rounds," added Lonan.

"I can lead a group of your men there," said Armon.

"We've completed as much recon of the camps as we can. The missions are planned, and now we're training the teams," reported Cloin.

"I have one more weapon I'm finishing now," said Lonan.

"OK, finish your assignments as soon as you can. We don't have much more time," commanded Kilgron.

As the group split up and went their separate ways, Armon pulled Ahren and Cloin aside.

"While I go get more armor, I need you to bring more of our soldiers here and prepare our home for lockdown."

"Yes, Father," answered Cloin and Ahren.

"Be on your guard. I sense that this battle will begin sooner than we expect," warned Armon.

Cloin and Ahren nodded in agreement.

Chapter 16

While the Helion and Seberian forces continued their preparations, Devakin and his group of Leviathan elite finished loading into a small Nemaron transport. The elite was a hand-selected group of twenty soldiers who were particularly powerful and ruthless. Devakin led this team personally. After loading all their weapons, they blasted off from the main hangar of the Nemaron command ship, on course for Helion.

In the main hangar, Sevran worked to finish mounting missile launchers on the sides of his motorcycle as Lonan and Telgrin finished bringing back all their equipment from the shooting range. As they entered the shop, Lonan received a transmission from the command center.

"There are sensors down in sector nineteen. Could you send someone to fix them?"

"Again? Yeah, I'll take care of it," answered Lonan as he turned off his com and turned to Telgrin.

"I'm going this time. I need to get some fresh air and clear my head. I've been cooped up here in the shop too long. And apparently no one else can get it right."

He picked up a tool pouch and walked to his waiting motorcycle and began loading tools. He also loaded several clips of the new electric rounds. Sevran looked up from working on his motorcycle and asked, "You're not going by yourself, are you?"

"No, I'll get some help." He turned to a soldier standing guard at the hangar door and said, "Corporal, grab a bike. I need your help."

The soldier immediately ran deeper into the hangar to get a motorcycle.

"Wait, I'll go with you," said Sevran.

"No, you have too much work to do. You've been slacking off while the rest of us have been working."

"What? I was in the medical bay taking care of patients," snapped Sevran as his face started to turn red.

Lonan smiled as he continued loading his bike. "I thought we were all given orders to work on vehicle and weapon conversion."

"What?" asked Sevran, who was so upset that he could hardly speak. Finally he calmed down when he realized he was being messed with. "You know that when I'm needed in the medical bay that takes priority over shop work." He relaxed his brow and went back to what he was doing.

Telgrin stood facing the other direction with a big smile on his face. He loved it when the brothers argued.

Just then the Helion soldier rolled up on his motorcycle, and Lonan threw his leg over his. He turned to Sevran and said, "I know you hide in there because you don't like to get your hands dirty out here with us." He started the engine before Sevran could respond.

Sevran stopped what he was doing and jumped to his feet as he tried to yell over the sound of the engine. "Hands dirty? Haven't you seen the blood and guts that I get covered in? What are you talking about, 'hands dirty'?"

Lonan threw on his helmet and lifted his hand to his ear, hinting that he couldn't hear his little brother. As Sevran walked in his direction, trying to yell over the sound of the two motorcycles, Lonan kicked his into gear and rode off through the open hangar door. The corporal followed behind.

As Sevran watched them ride out the door, he could see Telgrin laughing quietly to himself. Sevran wadded up the dirty rag he had in his hand and threw it at him.

"Shut up!"

Later that day, Ahren and Cloin arrived at their home high in the mountains of planet Seber. As they entered, they were greeted by two other soldiers while three children ran past as they played.

"Father wants all of our available soldiers on planet Helion," reported Cloin. "Leave a standard protection team here at the base."

"Of course."

They then each went their separate ways to tell everyone and prepare to move out.

Many kilometers away from the Helion base, in sector twenty, the small Nemaron transport flew just above the tops of the tall trees that covered the mountain ranges. They slowed and landed in a small clearing in the bottom of a valley. Once they landed, the back hatch opened, and all twenty Leviathan elite marched out, carrying massive rifles. Devakin followed them.

"Begin scanning the area, and jam all their transmissions. We walk in from here, but stay hidden; we don't want to draw their attention."

On the far side of the planet, Genon patrolled the outer atmosphere while riding his horse. Suddenly he pulled back on the reins and looked at the planet Helion. His eyes blazed with white light as he turned and flew back toward the planet.

Back on planet Seber, Cloin walked through the dining room with bags of weapons. Suddenly she stopped, and her eyes lit up. Just then Ahren stepped in the room with his eyes also ablaze.

"They're on Helion." They both walked out of the room and down the long hallway entrance. There another of the Seberian soldiers whose eyes were also bright white met them.

"Keep the families safe. The rest of us will find the enemy," ordered Cloin as they all stepped through the front door. The other nine soldiers were already kissing their wives and children goodbye as they loaded their weapons into a transport. Moments later they took off into the sky, on course for Helion.

Meanwhile Lonan and the Helion soldier had reached the malfunctioning sensor in sector nineteen and had started to work. The sensor was in a small valley that opened away from the base. It was a camouflaged dish-shaped sensor that slowly rotated on a base that housed all the electronics. It stood nearly two meters tall but was still blending into the surroundings well and could not easily be seen.

They had already disassembled much of the control panel in the base and were working to find out what had caused it to go offline. The soldier kept watch as he scanned the area and occasionally retrieved equipment from the motorcycle for Lonan.

"How did this happen?" Lonan asked as he popped his head out of the base of the sensor. "There is one circuit board that is completely fried and another that was cleanly disconnected. It almost looks like it was tampered with."

What they didn't know was that Devakin and his soldiers were very nearby, in the next valley across the large hill in front of them.

The Leviathan soldiers and Devakin moved quickly through the thick forest as they climbed up through a valley and came to a clearing on top of the nearby hill. From this position, they could see through the mountains and had a clear view of the Helion base off in the distance.

"Set up here, and get some readings. The rest of you secure the area," barked Devakin as he held scanning equipment to his eyes to get a closer look at the base.

Two of his soldiers set up a small tripod and placed a telescopic-looking piece of machinery on it. They then attached it to a small portable computer they carried in a hard case. They pointed the telescope in the direction of the base, and the computer immediately began scanning the entire mountain. Three-dimensional images of the outside and inside of the base began to appear on the screen.

The computer took measurements and completed calculations of every piece of the mountain base.

As Genon entered the inner atmosphere of planet Helion, Abaddon suddenly appeared from a shadow. He was mounted on his horse and flew directly across Genon's path. With his sword drawn, Abaddon reached out with a heavy swing, aiming for the angel's throat. Genon saw him barely in time and leaned back just far enough to avoid the demon's blade.

Abaddon circled back and said, "That was close. I nearly sent you home."

Abaddon then raised his sword and shot balls of fire, which Genon deflected as he quickly drew his shield. Abaddon moved in to attack again. As they collided in sword battle, sparks and flames flew in all directions. They both began to circle in a figure-eight flight pattern. As they met in the center, their blades and shields collided.

"I don't have time for this," Genon thought to himself as his eyes burned bright white.

On the next pass, he fired a tremendously large bolt of lightning from the tip of his sword, scorching Abaddon enough that he and his horse writhed in pain as they drifted off into space. That allowed Genon enough time to get away, and he flew quickly toward the planet.

Back in sector twenty, Devakin looked out across the valleys as one of his soldiers ran to him and reported, "We've found something, sir."

"Show me."

They walked down the heavily wooded hill awhile until they came to a spot where a narrow gully opened into a valley down below. Through the clearing that this created, they could see the two Helion motorcycles, but neither Lonan nor the soldier. Devakin lifted his scanning device to his eyes to get a closer look.

Just then the Helion soldier stepped into view as he walked to the motorcycle and rummaged through one of the storage compartments. He walked back toward Lonan, who was still trying to figure out what had happened to the sensor.

"It doesn't look like anyone broke into the control panel. I can't understand how this happened."

"Sorry, sir, but I don't either," said the corporal as he made his way back to Lonan with some tools. Suddenly three rounds silently flew down through the trees and into his chest.

The impact threw him backward, and he hit the ground. Lonan whipped his head around to find the man lying on his back. He rushed to him, pulled him behind one of the bikes, and checked his vitals. He was dead. Lonan hung his head as he tried to figure out his next move. Just then three more rounds came down from the hillside and hit the top of the bike he was hiding behind. They hit the computer console and took out the entire electrical system, including the communications.

"No! I've got to call for help," said Lonan as he looked at the other bike.

Just then a rocket came down from the enemy position and completely destroyed the second bike. Lonan ducked from the flying shrapnel. After the debris stopped falling, he looked over the top of the remaining bike. He could see Leviathan soldiers moving down the hill through the trees with their weapons drawn and pointed in his direction. He reached up and tried to turn on the side shield of the bike, but it had been destroyed.

He then manually pulled out the quad-barrel gun that deployed from the rear sides of the bike. He took careful aim and fired on the nearest Leviathan soldier. The round hit him and sent him flying backward several meters. It sent an electrical current all through his body as he lay on the ground unconscious.

The rest of the soldiers continued down the hill, completely unfazed by the fact that one of their men lay convulsing on the ground. Lonan fired another shot and hit another Leviathan. He fired a third shot, but this time they were aware and used their speed to dodge the electric rounds. He fired again. Some rounds they dodged while others they couldn't, and he took out two more of them.

As Lonan was taking aim again, he saw through his scope that one of the soldiers was ready to fire a rocket. He saw him pull the trigger as a blast exited the back of the launcher. Lonan jumped immediately, and a second later the last motorcycle burst into flames. He crawled over to his bag and hid behind the sensor platform. He filled his pockets with electric round clips and grabbed his rifle. He took aim and fired several rounds. Unfortunately each was dodged.

The enemy was drawing very near, so he crawled backward, down into a deeper gully. He then turned and looked up into the hills on the far side as he tried to find a better position. Several of the Leviathan soldiers slowly moved down and out of cover of the trees, into the narrow clearing of the valley. They had nearly reached the place where the remains of the two motorcycles lay smoking.

Just then two arrows flew down from the wooded hill on the opposite side of the gully. The Leviathan turned and returned fire but couldn't see anyone. They fired recklessly into the trees as the drugs began to affect them and they fell to the ground, unconscious. This drew the attention of the rest of the Leviathan as they poured down into the clearing. More arrows came from the trees and hit two more Leviathan. Moments later they too hit the ground. The rest of them fired into the trees in every direction.

While they were distracted, Lonan took the opportunity to move from his position in the gully and took out another Leviathan.

Suddenly someone grabbed him from behind and lifted him out of the gully and threw him across the clearing. His back slammed against a tree. When he collected himself enough to look up, he saw Devakin standing fifteen meters away.

"There you are. Hiding in a hole," sneered Devakin.

As Lonan had flown through the air, he had dropped his rifle, which now lay five meters away. He looked at it, as did Devakin. Lonan jumped to grab the rifle, but Devakin ran at such an incredible speed that he reached it first and kicked it into the trees. Lonan jumped to his feet and punched Devakin in the face twice. The impact had no effect on him. He responded by punching Lonan in the face, which sent him flying backward another fifteen meters.

"I hope you're not the best that your planet has to offer. If so, this will be far easier than we thought," jeered Devakin as he slowly walked toward Lonan.

Just then Cloin and the other nine Seberians flew down the hill at lightning speed. They attacked the Leviathan soldiers in hand-to-hand combat. Quickly they disarmed them and threw their rifles into the trees. The combat was so fast that Lonan could only see them as a blur. As he watched, he struggled to figure out if it was real or part of the spinning sensation in his head.

Devakin turned his attention back to Lonan and reached down to grab him when suddenly Ahren jumped from the trees and tackled him. They rolled on the ground as they fought until Ahren jumped to his feet and turned to face the giant before him. Devakin was at a definite size and strength advantage; however, Ahren quickly showed his opponent that he was not only faster but also better trained.

Chapter 17

On planet Malton, Armon and several Helion soldiers worked quickly to collect angel and demon armor. Off in the distance, they could see the ruins of the capital city where Lonan's parents had been killed. They rummaged through the wreckage of the battle from long ago and used heavy machinery to load the armor.

Three of the Helion soldiers drove the lifts as the others worked to roll the armor onto the machines' platforms. Armon was hunched over, loading armor, when suddenly he bolted upright with his eyes engulfed in white-hot light.

Great concern came to his face as he said, "I shouldn't be here. We need to go back—now!"

The Helion soldiers looked around in confusion as Armon ran back to the shuttle.

"Come on! We're going back!" he yelled.

The soldiers finished loading the pieces they had in their hands and quickly followed him back to the shuttle.

Back on planet Helion, Cloin and the other Seberian soldiers continued to battle the Leviathan at superhuman speeds. These particular Leviathan were extremely fast and powerful. They were able to withstand a tremendous beating without losing power.

Suddenly, what looked like a meteor fell from the sky. As it drew closer, the Seberian and Leviathan soldiers could see that it was Genon and Abaddon as they swirled around each other in battle. Their blades collided, and lightning and fire fell all around them. They dropped out of the sky and crashed in an open field down below the narrow gully in which Cloin and her men were fighting. As they hit the ground, dirt and ash flew fifteen meters into the air.

Lonan looked over to see what had landed while he tried to clear his head. His vision was blurry from his collision with the tree, so he wasn't sure what he was seeing. He could make out the dirt flying into the air, but that was all. He couldn't see the angel or the demon. He did, however, catch glimpses of shadows moving across the field.

Lonan looked down to see the right sleeve of his battle armor soaked in blood. He tried to move his arm but was quickly stopped by a gut-wrenching pain. Both his right arm and leg were badly broken.

Genon and Abaddon continued their battle on foot. Their blades and shields whirled through the air in fluid, balletic motion. Abaddon was larger and appeared to be more powerful; however, Genon's speed allowed him to land a very painful strike to the upper thigh of Abaddon's left leg. The blade laid open Abaddon's flesh, and black blood ran for only seconds before the wound began to heal. He limped back in pain.

"I will not be bloodied by a subordinate angel!"

"I'm no longer a subordinate to you," said Genon as he circled his opponent. "You forfeited your position with the decision you made long ago. 'To whom much is given, much will be expected,' and you failed."

With that, Genon continued his attack with renewed force. Abaddon struggled to defend himself against the onslaught.

"Because of you, many of my brothers died—or worse—were enslaved by your poison," said Genon as he wielded his blade in a flurry of light and wind.

Up in the gully, Cloin and her men continued their fight against the Leviathans who wouldn't tire or weaken. To remove the source of their power, the Seberians began to destroy and rip off the chest plates of the Leviathan armor. As they did, they exposed the demonic chest piece buried deep under their man-made battle armor.

The Seberians could see the piece had dug itself deep into the flesh of the Leviathans' chests. It surged with bright-red light. With their blades and well-placed punches, the Seberian soldiers gradually weakened the chest pieces until they were able to rip them from the Leviathans' bodies. The Leviathans cried out in immense pain as blood poured from the area where the teeth of the piece had been embedded in the skin. With great persistence and struggle, they pulled armor from the Leviathan, one by one.

As they did, each man fell to his knees and lay limp on the ground. The red light faded from their eyes, and they returned to a more human form. Once removed, the red light of the chest piece began to fade. The Seberians threw them to the ground and crushed them underfoot.

Farther up in the gully, Devakin and Ahren continued their battle. Devakin saw what was happening to his soldiers.

"I see that Armon has taught you a great deal about my men and from where they get their power. Has he told you how he knows so much about us?"

Ahren stopped his attack for a moment and stepped backward. He looked at Devakin with great confusion and concern. Cloin was near enough that she could overhear the conversation, and she also paused in her fight and turned her attention to Devakin.

"We don't question Father," answered Ahren.

"Maybe you should," returned Devakin with a grin.

He then pulled a blade from a leg harness and lunged at Ahren. His attack was so furious that Ahren could hardly defend himself. Suddenly Devakin plunged his half-meter-long blade into Ahren's stomach.

"No!" cried Cloin as she ran toward her brother.

Genon turned and looked when he heard her. He could feel that Ahren had been wounded.

Devakin picked Ahren up by the throat as he gasped for air. Devakin threw him across the clearing, where he hit a tree and fell to the ground very near to Lonan. The Seberian soldiers all ran to engage Devakin as they stood between him and the place where Ahren lay. Cloin ran to his side and found him bleeding very badly. Lonan dragged himself with his one good arm over to try to help.

"Stay with me. You're going to be OK," said Cloin as she pulled bandages from a small pack on her back and began applying pressure to his wound.

Ahren pulled his hand from his stomach to find it covered in blood.

"That doesn't look good," moaned Ahren.

Cloin's face was locked in a stoic intensity as she ignored his comment and she focused on trying to stop the bleeding.

"Leave me alone. I'll be fine."

"No, you need my help."

"Cloin," he said as he grabbed her hands. She stopped but didn't look up at him. "I think that my time here is done."

She slowly looked up to his eyes as the intensity drained from her face.

"Don't worry," he said as he winced in pain. "I'll be alright and at peace."

After a few seconds' hesitation, she went back to work dressing his wound.

Ahren turned to Lonan and said, "Listen to me. You must let go of the pain. He is good. It is not His fault."

Lonan looked into his eyes and saw great tranquility that he couldn't understand. Not only could he not understand it, but for some reason, it also disturbed him. Ahren turned back to his sister as blood began to run from the corner of his mouth.

"Take care of Father. Tell him thank you and that I love him."

Then Ahren slowly released his last breath.

Cloin stared in disbelief for a moment as she knelt beside her brother. She gently reached over and closed his eyes. Slowly she bowed her head and sat silently for a moment.

Lonan lay beside Ahren and watched as Cloin began to clench her fists. Suddenly she jumped to her feet. Her eyes burned bright as she slowly turned to face the battle that continued behind her. The last two Leviathan had joined the fight as Devakin held all nine Seberian soldiers at bay.

Cloin rushed in to join the battle. She directed all her energy at Devakin. She and five other Seberians engaged him in sword battle. The other four teamed up against the remaining two Leviathan. The speed and power of Devakin was tremendous. No one was able to land a successful blow. Suddenly he caught Cloin with a punch that sent her tumbling to the ground. As she struggled to get up, Devakin raised his right arm as he prepared to bring his blade down on her neck.

But suddenly an arrow pierced his outstretched arm. It passed through all his armor and caused him to drop his blade. He roared in pain as he turned to see Genon standing on the far side of the gully and holding his bow.

Behind him Abaddon charged in with his blade held high. Genon spun around just in time and blocked the thrust of the demon.

This gave Cloin a moment to collect herself and rejoin the fight.

Off along the edge of the trees, Lonan struggled to lift his rifle with his left arm. He winced in pain as he worked to prop it onto his one good knee. He took careful aim and fired. The shot was good, and he took out one more of the two remaining Leviathan.

As Devakin saw another of his soldiers fall, he knew that he would lose the battle. He pressed a button on his chest plate, extending a mask over his face.

"Tell your father I'll see him again very soon."

With that, he dropped a gas grenade, which covered the clearing with poison gas. This sent Cloin and the Seberians running up into the trees for clean air as they pulled masks from pouches on their backs.

Devakin and the one remaining Leviathan took their chance to escape. They fled up the hill and through the trees at an incredible speed.

Cloin walked slowly to her brother's body. She knelt beside him and gently rested her head against his. As she sat silently, she shed a single tear.

Lonan looked on in anguish, knowing there was nothing he could do.

The nine Seberian soldiers gathered their weapons and pursued Devakin. They ran up the hill so quickly that they caught up with the remaining Leviathan. He turned and opened fired as they followed. They dodged his rounds and then returned fire with tranquilizing arrows. Seconds later he hit the ground.

Genon and Abaddon continued evenly matched in their sword battle until Balim flew down on his horse. With the odds now two against one, Abaddon quickly decided to withdraw. His horse appeared. He mounted it and flew up into the sky, where he turned to face the angels.

"Your time has come to an end. We're gathering all our forces, and you'll not be able to withstand the power of our army."

With that, he flew off into space while the angels turned to tend to the humans.

Seconds later a Helion transport landed in the clearing at the bottom of the gully. Sevran and Telgrin ran up the hill with twenty other soldiers, who secured the area and searched for enemy soldiers.

"They're gone," said Lonan as Sevran ran to the place where he and Ahren lay.

Sevran gently pulled Cloin away from her brother and said, "Let me try to help him."

"It's too late," said Lonan, making eye contact with his brother.

Cloin stepped aside. She turned and looked up the hill at Genon and Balim, who were just stepping over the ridge. The angels' eyes were filled with the deepest sadness. They bowed their heads in respect to the fallen warrior as Cloin shed just one more tear.

Sevran examined Ahren and checked his vital signs. Moments later he turned to Cloin and said, "I'm sorry."

The Seberians continued on through the forest to stop Devakin. He was very far ahead of them and had already reached the clearing where they had set up their scanning equipment. As he ran through the clearing, he didn't stop but quickly grabbed the computer and continued on down the hill to his waiting shuttle.

He climbed on board and was in the air in moments. The Seberians arrived to see the cargo-bay door close and the engines blast as he headed into the atmosphere.

Back at the base, the Helion shuttle landed in the clearing in front of the main hangar. The cargo-bay ramp slowly lowered as Averine and several medics ran to greet them. The mood was somber as the soldiers brought Ahren's body out on a floating stretcher that was covered with a black sheet.

Averine looked at it with horror, fearing it was her husband. She was filled with relief when she saw him conscious and sitting on another stretcher. His arm and leg had both been placed in electronic casts that were scanning and monitoring his injuries. His head and abdomen were wrapped in bandages. She ran to meet him as Kilgron hobbled through the hangar door. He was noticeably relieved to see Lonan alive.

"Are you OK?" asked Averine as she examined him.

"He has a broken arm and leg. Nearly all his ribs are cracked, and, of course, he has a serious concussion," answered Sevran.

"What happened?" asked Averine.

"A lot," said Lonan as he looked at Cloin, who was walking behind the stretcher that carried her brother's body. The rest of the Seberian soldiers walked beside her. She stared with a stoic gaze at the black sheet that covered her brother.

Sevran stepped beside Cloin and quietly said, "I'm sorry about your bother. He seemed like a great man."

She kept her gaze on her brother and said, "Yes, he was." Then she looked up and into Sevran's eyes. "Thank you."

Just then another shuttle landed, and Armon jumped out before it even touched the ground. Cloin turned and walked to him as he ran toward the stretcher.

"Father, it's Ahren," she said.

"What happened?" he asked.

Armon slowly walked to the stretcher and placed his hand on Ahren's leg. He bowed his head in pain as he pulled Cloin close and hugged her.

Lonan gently added, "He died defending me. There were at least twenty Leviathan. They killed one of my men and would have killed me if they hadn't shown up when they did."

He turned to Cloin and said, "Thank you."

She nodded her head, as did the rest of the Seberian soldiers. The Helion medics pushed Lonan into the hangar and to the medial bay as Averine continued to monitor the medical system.

"Father, it was Devakin who killed Ahren. He asked some strange questions about you. He spoke as if he knew you," said Cloin.

The greatest intensity came to Armon's eyes as he said, "That man's thirst for blood will never end. It's time for something to be done."

"Father, what are you talking about?"

"There are many things I have not told you. Maybe the time has come," answered Armon as they followed the stretcher into the base.

In the medical bay, two medics helped Lonan off the floating stretcher and onto a bed. The rest of the bay was filled with the rescued slaves from the Tarnus camp. Most of them were unconscious and hooked up to many different machines.

"OK, let's start with your leg," said Averine as she examined the electronic cast.

Just then the little girl from the Tarnus camp ran into the medical bay with her rag doll. She looked around the room, searching for her parents.

"Hey, is that the kid from Tarnus?" asked Lonan as his eyes lit up.

"Some of the captives are finally coming to. She's been searching everywhere for her parents," answered Averine.

Lonan turned to Averine and, with deep concern in his voice, asked, "Did we get them?"

"I don't know."

As they talked, the girl ran from bed to bed, scanning the faces and trying to see under the bandages of the unconscious people lying on the beds. Lonan watched her with great concern. Suddenly she found a face that she recognized.

"Daddy!" she yelled as she ran and jumped on the bed of her unconscious father. She shook him and called him until he finally woke up.

"Hey, little one. Are you OK?" he asked as he looked around, trying to figure out where he was.

They hugged, and she kissed his bandaged cheek.

"Yeah, I'm fine, but I can't find mommy," she said as she looked around. Suddenly she cried out, "Mommy!"

She jumped off the bed, ran across the room, and leapt onto her mother's bed. She too was bandaged and sleeping. She woke up very confused, but her daughter quickly filled her in on what had happened. Her husband crawled from his bed and hobbled across the room. They greeted each other with a hug, and then all three sat on the bed together.

"Where are we?" she asked.

"I don't know."

Sevran stepped into the medical bay just in time to hear her question.

"Don't worry; you're safe. Just rest and let your bodies recover. You were all in pretty bad shape."

He then walked to the bed where Averine was examining his brother.

"The kid you rescued is OK," said Lonan.

"Actually, we both had a hand in that. Give yourself some credit."

Sevran smiled and patted Lonan on the shoulder, which caused him to wince in pain.

"Whoops, sorry. Wow, he really messed you up, didn't he?"

Averine stepped in and pushed Sevran away from the bed.

"OK, leave him alone," she said.

Lonan wasn't paying much attention to his brother. He watched with great peace in his eyes as the family from Tarnus hugged each other.

"See, you did some good, and it made a difference for them," whispered Averine.

"Yeah, I see. And I got you two home safely."

"Yes, thank you for that, by the way."

"You're welcome," said Lonan as he turned and grinned at his wife. "Finally. It's nice to be apprecia—Ouch!" cried Lonan as Averine pushed on his broken ribs. "Take it easy. You know those are broken."

"I'm sorry," said Averine as she looked away with a grin.

Meanwhile at the Nemaron command ship, Devakin brought his shuttle in for a landing in one of the smaller hangars. He exited the ship with the computer. From there he left the hangar and walked through the hallways.

Moments later he arrived at a large balcony that overlooked one of the largest hangars. Maginon was there looking out across the ships down below.

"I trust you have the data."

"Yes," answered Devakin.

He stepped forward and handed the computer to Maginon, who turned and handed it to one of his soldiers.

"Good. Then we are ready for our attack," said Maginon as he smiled and looked down over the thousands of Leviathan soldiers marching in formation as they entered large transport ships.

On Satan's lair planet, hundreds of thousands of Leviathan soldiers marched up from caverns into a wide valley, where they stood in formation. There they waited to load into the Nemaron transports that were scattered across the dusty valley.

Hundreds of demons flew in the ash-filled air above them and shouted orders as more and more men poured onto the surface of the planet from the deep caverns below.

Here ends the first part of the history of the alliance formed between the planet Helion and the Seberians. The second part tells of the great battle between the Angels and Demons at the portal to Heaven in Seberian, The Great Gate